DESCENT
INTO NIGHT

Edem Awumey

translated by
Phyllis Aronoff & Howard Scott

Mawenzi
House

©2013 by Éditions du Boréal
published in a French edition as *Explication de la nuit*
English language translation Copyright ©2017 Phyllis Aronoff & Howard Scott

We acknowledge the support of the Canada Council for the Arts for our publishing program. We also acknowledge support from the Government of Ontario through the Ontario Arts Council.

We acknowledge the financial support of the Government of Canada through the National Translation Program for Book Publishing, an initiative of the *Roadmap for Canada's Official Languages 2013-2018: Education, Immigration, Communities*, for our translation activities.

ONTARIO ARTS COUNCIL
CONSEIL DES ARTS DE L'ONTARIO
an Ontario government agency
un organisme du gouvernement de l'Ontario

Canada Council   Conseil des arts
for the Arts   du Canada

Cover design by Sabrina Pignataro

Cover photo from Morguefile.com

Author photo by Steve Arnold

Library and Archives Canada Cataloguing in Publication

Awumey, Edem, 1975-
[Explication de la nuit. English]
            Descent into night / Edem Awumey ; translated by
Phyllis Aronoff & Howard Scott.

Translation of: Explication de la nuit.
Issued in print and electronic formats.
ISBN 978-1-988449-16-6 (softcover).--ISBN 978-1-988449-21-0 (HTML)

            I. Aronoff, Phyllis, 1945-, translator II. Scott, Howard, 1952-,
translator III. Title. IV. Title: Explication de la nuit. English.

PS8601.W86E9613 2017   C843'.6   C2017-904513-X

                                                   C2017-904514-8

Printed and bound in Canada by Coach House Printing

Mawenzi House Publishers Ltd.
39 Woburn Avenue (B)
Toronto, Ontario M5M 1K5
Canada

www.mawenzihouse.com

For the dead . . .
and a few of the living, luminous with madness

To Kossi Efoui

Any resemblance between this fiction and any reality would be very interesting . . . and sad.

But now I'm at home, sitting on a chair, my head drooping lower and lower, until I drift off the only way I know how, moist lips against raised knees.

BOHUMIL HRABAL, Too Loud a Solitude

1

His nose pressed to the window of the train speeding through a world bleached white in the darkness of the night, Ito Baraka thinks back to the scene he has been rehearsing for days now. He stops in the middle of the basement that is his home. He looks up and examines the ceiling fan. He studies the housing and he thinks to himself that if he doesn't have a rope, he'll have to cut the sleeves off some shirts.

He looks at the fan with its rusty blades stilled, useless now, in a crumbling ceiling, and remembers his country and a failed spring. He hasn't forgotten that on day three of their strike, the government sent the army onto the campus. Jeeps had taken possession of the space for three days, surveilling their flock of obstinate little intellectuals. Then, on the fourth day, the army charged, going after the leaders of the protest. It was a fine hunt, leopards chasing zebras in the wilderness, with beatings, clubs casually cracking skulls, stampedes in the corridors of the dormitories, arms and legs dismembered, the uniformed thugs tracking down their friend Neto, the vise closing tighter and tighter around him. Neto had chosen that nickname in memory of his idol, the Angolan poet and revolutionary Agostinho Neto. Because they were still at that age when you need gods. Ito Baraka hasn't forgotten. Many years later, slumped on his sofa, he sees it all again, how the army finally cornered Neto on the third floor of the dormitory. On one side, the left, a window and a streaked sky.

Ito Baraka wants to be done with that past. Alone in his apartment, he rehearses the suicide scene. He looks for his scissors to cut off the shirt sleeves. Then he'll just have to tie a good slipknot and let himself go. It will be a way, the final way, to put an end to the brutal invasion of those images that have so often kept him from closing his eyes, the vise closing around Neto trapped beside the window in the surrounded dorm, the kick of a boot, the glass shattering into a thousand sharp shards. The film is cruelly clear before Ito's eyes. The army rearranges Neto's face, uppercuts swelling his temples, uprooting his nose, and splitting his brow open. They lift the young man, who sees the shivering tops of the trees. The imperturbable majesty of the eucalyptus trees around the dorm, the ugly clouds, the corridor and the window floating, the impassive sky, and Neto thrown out the window. A hoarse scream, the scream of the little shit of a leader falling onto the hard ochre earth in the dormitory yard, a slick of blood around his head, a halo of sainthood won by the martyr with dilated pupils. Ito Baraka remembers, he was among the student rebels standing around their comrade's body, its limbs twitching in a macabre dance, while the soldiers continued combing the corridors of the dorm looking for other black sheep. "A taxi," shouted a girl in the group of students around poor half-dead Neto as his body's dance came to an end with the death rattle of an ancient record player.

Ito and the others stood powerless looking at their fallen friend, the slick of blood becoming a pool, the lips of the dying man mumbling incoherent words, the first description and mapping of the beyond delivered still warm to those who, for the time being, were still among the living. Someone whistled, the army retreating, the taxi they found twenty minutes later, the hospital corridors strewn with other disjointed puppets. "Put him down there," a man in a white coat said coldly. In the middle of the night, a doctor finally arrived, who shook his head as soon as he saw the poor guy. Ito thought of the rag doll his mother had made for him on her Singer sewing machine, that first companion he dragged around for a long time, holding on to it by one arm, and his mother's warning, "If you pull him apart, I won't be able to sew him up again quickly enough and he'll die." And since it was only then that the doctor arrived, he wondered whether the scalpels and the scissors had come too late for Neto.

The doctor sent them away and shut himself up inside an operating room with the dying man. When they came back the next day, they were told, "You have to wait, still in the operating room," and in the following hours, "In post-op." On the third day, "Coma," and then for weeks on end, "Coma," until they were forbidden to visit for some obscure reason, something about visits being restricted to the immediate family. Ito Baraka doesn't know what became of the boy. That year it was hard to count the dead, the wounded, and the disappeared on campus, as order and fear returned to the amphitheatres with their shattered windows.

Ito Baraka, in his basement, rehearses the final scene. He glances at the fan overhead, he stands on his sofa, which creaks. He has a hard time keeping his balance because of the broken springs. He tosses the rope, which catches in the blades of the fan, and pulls on it. What comes next? Tie the knot with the end he's holding. Then he senses his friend Koli Lem's hand gripping his arm in the cell in the camp where they were held, back in his country, a nice knot right where Koli's long fingers are pressing Ito's flesh, and hears Koli whisper, "Don't worry, we'll get out of here, and with everything you've been through, you'll become a great writer, you'll be Aleksandr Solzhenitsyn!"

Yes, Koli assured him in that place of dying lost deep in the sun-scorched savannah, Ito Baraka will be a famous and sadly painful writer, and as with his characters, he will choose the end he wants for himself. He will choose the time and the weapon and his last thought, and he will die at the height of his glory in his basement, in this apartment that is itself a tomb for the sun.

In their tropical prison, Koli Lem was still whispering, "You'll be Yukio Mishima!" It is this time of prison, this century of all the madness and all the fiascos that Ito Baraka is trying to recount in a book, his last one, with what remains to him of blood and fleeting memory.

In the train bringing him back from Quebec City, where he was invited to give a reading in front of an indifferent audience, the face of his fellow prisoner continues to intrude on him, with Koli repeating, "You will be Garcia Lorca!" Yes, Ito Baraka will be—in what future?— a flamboyant artist or just a guy who disturbs people, and one joyful morning at dawn, in an empty yard, he will, like Garcia Lorca, be dressed in his final suit with a dandy's stripes. They'll make a wall of his books, stand him in front of it, and shoot him!

2

The train is a long reptile slithering through the night jungle. Ito Baraka hunkers down in his seat. To anyone who happens to walk through the empty wagon at that particular moment, he will appear a shady character, an old pile of skin and bones covered with a coat that's too big and makes him look like a fallen god. Through the closed window, he thinks he can make out eyes peering at him, the inquisitive gaze of big black cats, cruel creatures whose claws are raking his flesh. He looks like Hamm, the grumpy blind old cripple in Beckett's play *Endgame*. He thinks about Hamm, and about Beckett, because that's where it all started for him.

The train is a noise and a dull ache running through his veins. He coughs and bends down and grabs the backpack between his legs. He starts to take out his big notebook, but then changes his mind and pulls from the inside pocket of his coat the flask he always carries, and takes a sip from it. His hands trembling, he gets out the notebook, opens it in the middle, and begins to read. He shivers. He knows he won't have time to complete this book. He reads over the paragraph he finished when the train pulled out of Quebec City.

——— ♦ ———

Nineteen eighty. There would continue to be only one way of thinking in the country, in keeping with the directives of the party. I remember we had to stand stiff-necked, all looking in the same direction, the direction of the wind, and after long days of immobility, our joints would ache, and an army general would appear out of nowhere and make us turn our heads in another direction, the direction of emptiness. And my father didn't see how we could survive between those two poles of wind and emptiness. In our neighbourhood there was an old man they called the Walker, a wretched creature scarred by a series of failures and misfortunes. He would walk the streets of the neighbourhood heaping insults on everyone he met, calling the passersby wimps, losers, nutless, gutless, goddamn niggers, jackasses. At six in the morning, we'd hear the guy in the north end of the neighbourhood, and his voice would gradually move towards us and his volley of insults would once again disturb the more sensitive of the good citizens and fail to impress the old people, who had been through it all, and worse, since the sky of lead and misery had fallen on our heads. And they pronounced the man a madman and philosopher and said he'd spent twenty years in jail for affront to public decency, slander, treason, and other crimes. And the better informed of our fellow-citizens confirmed that he had said things against the powers-that-be, nobody knew exactly what, and one day a sergeant and his detachment came out of the watchtowers of the city and tossed him in jail. There are watchtowers there, right in the middle of the city. Watchtowers, army camps, men in fatigues, green jeeps, and a sergeant sitting in the rear seat of his patrol car, an Uzi across his skinny chicken legs. Also airplanes in a gloomy sky.

Very often, my father, a surveyor who worked in the fields with his tripod and transit and other optical instruments, would catch sight of a flying object in the sky. It might be an army helicopter doing reconnaissance on our hotheads, and my father, to avoid trouble, would move his field of observation, while the neighbourhood madman continued insulting us in his voice of an opera singer who has seen better days, the shrill notes of rage and frustration finally catching in his throat, cutting off his breath, and throwing him against a wall darkened with the piss and spittle of idlers. His words were the morning refrain that answered the crowing of a noisy rooster perched on the roof of the neighbourhood movie theatre. The Walker, calling us chickens, toadies, and losers, philosophizing about what he called our duck walk, ranting that we would never get further than the boundaries of our henhouse-neighbourhood, drawing a parallel between our daily promenade of the living dead and the gait of the few web-footed birds that strayed into the Bé lagoon. And he walked fast, exhorting passersby loud and clear to join the ranks of what he called The Revolution, the real one and not the one of the men in fatigues who had gotten us into such deep shit. The man would raise his fist, his whole body stiff. My father didn't want me to end up like him if that's what philosophizing was, asking for trouble and a boot in the ass! I enrolled in philosophy anyway, and got into Plato, Kant, Merleau-Ponty, and Sartre. My favourite, though, was Diogenes the Cynic, because, like him, the swindling brats around the dumps at the Train Station Market would search in broad daylight for light, light that was irremediably corrupted by the veil of cruelty covering their malaria-yellowed eyes.

3

At night, I would sleep with my wise men and madmen from Athens, Rome, and the Age of Enlightenment, books by Plato, Aristotle, Marcus Aurelius, Rousseau, and Kant strewn on my bedding. I would read by candlelight—it was expensive to leave the fluorescent light on for long—at the risk of burning the mosquito netting, along with my notebooks, the mattress, and the whole sleeping household. I had made some friends at the university, two guys and a girl who were to be important in my little life. Beno and Wali were in the faculty of arts and Sika was studying law. We would spend entire afternoons at Beno's place remaking the world. A broken world, in fragments scattered on the little low table around which we sat talking, trying to glue together the pieces, the shards of shattered lives and dreams. That was before the riots and the crises that came one after the other, the crises and the outbursts of violence that had begun to reinvent death with a hole in the chest, a stiff on a sidewalk perforated like a target that impatient children or sharpshooters at a circus or fair have emptied their slugs into, a corpse of a girl with a hole between her breasts.

We led ordinary student lives between classes, books, flirtations that quickly petered out into boredom, and watching the turbulence of the ocean in the evening, when it wasn't yet sending back swollen corpses. However, later things were different, and there were fire and long knives shining during that night of massacres and summary executions. My father could no longer study things in the distance with his surveyor's theodolites or observe the pitching of the fishermen's boats moving towards the open sea. Instead, in his comings and goings at the outskirts of the city, he would come across what he called charcoal bodies—people burned and abandoned in sinister dead ends in which nothing could survive but fat, glutted black flies. My father would tear his eyes away, rub them with the palm of a trembling hand, and glue them back onto his instrument, and another human form, it too charred, would come into view on a vacant lot. And he would try to guess if it was a man or a woman. Very often, the charcoal body would have its mouth open and my father would conclude that the person should have kept it shut.

That was well after the university years, when we already sensed the hellish time coming and would talk about it in our discussions at our friend Beno's house. Beno's father, a teacher, thought we were studying for our exams, to him we were still well-behaved, disciplined youngsters, and it's true our long, impassioned debates were harmless. There was never a real blow-up. But soon there would be, with explosions in the neighbourhoods of the city. The TV spoke of terrorism and attempts to undermine the gains of peace and security, the fraudulent peace sold on our airwaves as the feat of the century. But death was beginning to freeze the faces of the most reckless. The Angel of Repression had begun prowling the alleys and the bars where we would go drinking to defy the fear, the invisible Angel portrayed in caricature wearing a helmet and holding a grenade with its pin permanently pulled, ready to trash any area or activity suspected of being contrary to the Nouvelle Marche, the new destiny defined by mutual agreement of all the active elements of the nation when the men in fatigues took power. We learned to know the Angel when we were shut up at Beno's place in our circle of young *poètes maudits* discussing fiery, iconoclastic works of Allen Ginsberg or Ezra Pound. We rubbed shoulders with the Angel until the day in February 1988 when the Faculty of Arts at the university invited a writer from the Congo, Sony Labou Tansi, who I remember had, somewhere around Brazzaville, come up with the sentence "A word is a dead body that aspires to resurrection." Writing as a matter of dead flesh that you stroke with your pen in order to get a sound, an echo, out of it. That image floated in my mind. I saw the writer pushing a cart and picking up bodies in the streets of imagination, death with a bluish sheen, adorned with a necklace of shiny flies and pearls, with macabre beauty marks and blowtorch burns or bullet holes in a body reduced to a torso. In the middle of his presentation to the students, Sony said, "Let's not remain silent, let's speak up, they won't do anything to us!" They wouldn't serve up our grilled testicles and guts to the generals with the finest wines at the next dinner on the calendar of the nation. His words resonated, as if a breach had been opened up in a reinforced concrete sky, and like wound-up clocks we were driven to act, to find a way to enter the corpses of the words Sony had resuscitated. We imagined it wouldn't be very complicated. Each dead body left on the asphalt of our revolution was pierced with holes of different sizes, holes through which we would penetrate those bodies and breathe life into them. But my father said, "He's nuts, your Sony, this is not a game!" For days after the man left, we talked longer and longer, until dawn, in Beno's little room, and from our refuge to the street it was just one step.

4

The railway car is desperately empty. The train slows down as it approaches an urban area. Ito Baraka feels a need to talk to someone. It's an old habit of his, spending the night talking to whoever cares to listen, a buddy or, very often, a woman, his muse of the moment, with whom he has just gone a first round of lovemaking. He'll talk to her until she regains her strength and mounts him again, and on the creaking bed he'll become a steed charging across the desert in search of a waterhole. And sometimes he finds that wellspring, when his friend of the evening starts to come and floods him. Then he feels himself come back to life, as if he has been baptized on the shores of a purifying river. And his eyelids grow heavy and he closes his eyes, the desert sand pulls him down, and his body becomes light, ethereal, like the bodies of the flying men.

It was his friend Koli Lem who first told him the story of the flying men. The story, or rather the mythology, of those who, back in his country in the north, were both feared and respected because they were not ordinary beings. Sorcerers, who had strange powers, and who, in their beds after nightfall, would close their eyes and order their spirits to leave their bodies and fly to distant lands. Strange beings with their arms outstretched above the sleeping huts, their wings of fire spread wide in the wind, they would soar upward and set a course for a land somewhere between the cardinal points, not as tourists, but to seek knowledge, to glean in that place at the ends of the earth the learning that made them what they were . . . soothsayers, magicians, healers, and above all, sorcerers and soul-eaters. They would go there and meet others of their kind, wizards, fakirs, and magicians, with whom they would talk all night long while taking part in strange rituals in which they tested their powers against each other, and banquets and orgies where wine, sperm, and blood overflowed from chalices and open skulls. And before first light, they would return sated and calm and re-enter their bodies and continue to live among ordinary people. At night, only the flying men could dream and enjoy life, only they knew the streets of the world in their entirety, the streets of the world and everything beautiful, horrible, or insignificant that happened there. They would come back among us with the conviction that they alone possessed the meaning of things.

Ito Baraka's dream is to become a flying man and from time to time to escape his painful body and his rotten blood that is taking him inexorably to the end.

He scrunches down a little more in his seat, breathing noisily. On his knees, the notebook he cherishes like a serious schoolboy, or one putting on an act for parents he considers gullible. He runs a trembling hand over the greasy, dog-eared pages. He should try to sleep, but because these moments are clearly a race against death, he lines up more words, bent over the page.

—— ♦ ——

At that time, the end of the 1980s, we were at the onset of a kind of fever. In the streets and markets and on theatre stages, we were dreaming with our eyes closed, envisioning the architecture of the country to come. Newspapers of every stripe were sketching the vague outlines of a state under the rule of law, freedom of speech, and human development.

However, those who had the balls to write in the newspapers would often get beaten up or, worse, gunned down. So it was necessary to find an indirect way to say these things that displeased the cops. We thought again of Sony and his theatre, and in a tiny space cleared in the middle of Beno's bedroom, we started acting out characters, King Lear, Ubu, Toussaint Louverture, tyrants or heroes in jail in France, Kamchatka, or the Congo. We would get into the skins of these characters to test ourselves as actors. We found acting fun, and we would be bent double laughing at our clownishness. And we came to the conclusion that if this acting and these gestures made us laugh like little kids, we wouldn't be so bad reinventing our lives on stage. And one morning, Beno, Wali, Sika, and I came up with a plan to create what would now be our reality, in which we could shout what we wanted without fear of reprisals by the sergeant with the Uzi. We decided to write a powerful play with four characters, with a role for each of us. That last point was a constraint, but we would be able to manage it, confident in our dazzling project, or blinded by it. We were thinking about this play when Wali borrowed from the university library a Beckett play we hadn't read yet, *Endgame.* And it happened that chance favoured our crazy ideas, and the play contained three male roles and one female. It was us, we were in the same immovable shit as Beckett's characters. And with that thought, I recalled some words of Beckett's in *Molloy* and I remembered the neighbourhood madman from my childhood who barraged us with songs and jokes all day long as though he understood those words by Beckett: "When you are in shit up to your neck, there is nothing left to do but sing." Yes, we were in shit, and that was why, as the nutcase declared, we smiled constantly in the city streets, clowns and parrots tirelessly repeating the same gestures and drivel, and when tourists landed in our city, they could observe our legendary good humour. In shit, and congregating in the squares downtown for the most comical of carnivals.

We were in deep shit, which was why the entire populace had to sing and dance when the country played host to a distinguished guest or some elected official, monarch, or despot wearing a suit and a few tacky medals, the people forming an honour guard from the airport to the presidential palace, school children, bureaucrats, teachers, newborns on the backs of the little mothers who didn't want to miss one bit of the hilarious show, and sorcerers and all the saints of the city, gesticulating and belting out the song of eternal tropical happiness. And I didn't yet understand that it was because we were in shit up to our ears that there was nothing left for us to do but this, to keep up a pretense as a form of resistance. I reread *Molloy*, and at the same time we assigned the roles in *Endgame*. Sika took the only female character, Nell, the old woman stuck in a trashcan like her old husband, Nagg, whom I was to play. I had it easy because I didn't have a lot of lines to learn, just had to stick my head up occasionally from my trashcan, my final dwelling place, and pester the two other male characters, who had a lot more crap to mouth. Hamm, the blind man, was played by Wali in a wheelchair, so it was clear that, physically, Wali would not have to make too much effort. And Beno took the role of the servant and caretaker, Hamm's adopted son, Clov, who went back and forth between the stage and the kitchen in the wings. And Hamm's old parents in the trashcans slept or sighed.

5

I remember the easy parallel we drew between the old people in
Beckett's play and the human wrecks and relics in the streets of our
city, in front of the houses, coughing and sighing, worn out, finished,
ruins of wrinkled flesh with the toothless expressions of zombies, their
mouths gaping open to frighten kids tarrying on the way to school.
We started rehearsing at Beno's place in the heavy heat of the afternoons when we had no classes and on the beach on weekends, offering our voices to the open sea. As I said, Sika and I didn't have a lot to
do inside our blue plastic trashcans. I would doze off, lulled by a sad,
monotonous swell, and so would Sika, I suppose, but at regular intervals Clov, I mean Beno, would give the barrels a kick to wake us up,
and in so doing, he was deviating from the stage directions. We pro-
gressed speech by speech, and thus, little by little our acting took form.
Hamm-Wali, in his chair that couldn't roll in the sand on the beach,
gave Clov-Beno a hard time, and the sand also hampered Clov-Beno's
movements. We would rehearse for hours, an audience of onlookers
forming a circle around us, though we didn't know as yet if we would
try to present the play on one of the stages in the capital.

We were not unhappy on the beach, wrapped as we were in an aura
of grandiloquent pride. Beyond the fact that it had four characters, we
had chosen *Endgame* because we saw it as a means to portray what
urgent, young, resolutely committed voices in the darkness of bars and

maquis, clandestine restaurants, and the corridors of our university were calling immobility, imprisonment, the status quo, the suspension of our movements on the stage of the single party. But I must say that the time we spent with our Beckett on the beach was above all a time of pleasure, at least until we left the text behind to go back to the unchanging theatre of the streets and crossroads, where the numbers of beggars and madmen had increased. In our performance we tried to add a little tropical flavour to the play. Hamm would hold onto his wheelchair and sink slowly down into the worn seat like a doddering king in the autumn of a thirty-year reign, his ass taking root in the throne, farting regularly and enveloping us in his tear gas, dulling the brilliance of our pretentious boldness from behind his blind man's dark glasses, coughing, dying a slow death, his legs inert, wearing not commando boots anymore but innocuous slippers. And because we were on the seashore, he would gradually sink into the sand up to his ears and the sea birds would come and pluck out his dead eyes.

6

Revolution, Ito Baraka says to himself, is a big word, a terrible horned beast that snatches and swallows up whatever it wants, especially lives, with all they contain of flesh and bone, blood and voice. It's that time when he and his partners in crime were devoured by the Beast that he's trying to find in his notebook, that time that both saddens and fascinates him, like an old possession you want to take out of a trunk to see if it will have the same effect on you that it once did or if its beauty could have been deceptive to your fevered gaze of long ago. Because all that is far away now, like the last stifled sob of his mother in the airport departure lounge the day he left the country. That was twenty years ago. Maybe more. He tries to revive that monster they had called Revolution in the fervor of young hearts and the turmoil in the streets.

Ito Baraka rouses himself. He wonders if he will be able to tell it all. He knows it will depend on his body, which is trying to trace the contours of other faces and voices, men and women lost in the mists of the past. He knows he will be able to do it if his body holds up long enough. Because soon the fever and the cold will try to regain the upper hand. Then, to get warm, he'll rub his body with his trembling hands, he'll rub his skin and bones so as to stay here with us long enough to finish his story. You live well and long if the light body of night allows you to dream and take flight. That's what his friend

Koli Lem would repeat during the long hours of tropical time. On the other hand, you croak pretty fast in the cellars of torture and pain, like Albert Ayler with his trumpet in a gutter in America, his jacket dirty, and shit on his skin, or like a poet, Paul Celan or Gherasim Luca, in a night flight from a bridge on the Seine. You die like that, at a turning point in life when the body that carries you is one of pain, anguish, insomnia.

The train, thinks Ito Baraka, must be travelling under a clear sky. You might even be able to catch sight of the flying men in the sky. His friend Koli Lem would tell how the flying men came back feeling light from their nocturnal journeys in the air. Relieved of all anxiety, fear, and pain, they simply went back to living instead of exhausting them-selves like the tormented *poètes maudits* searching for the meaning of life and of what was happening within them and around them. Instead of trying to disassemble and reassemble the mechanism of reality in the hope of understanding it. "They're making a mistake," declared his friend Koli Lem, "the mechanism of reality doesn't change, it's a sturdy, well-oiled machine. It's in the head that something's not right, some-thing snapped a long time ago. Like a poet or a madman, you've been hanging out in the streets and the shadowy nights of the world, trying to console yourself with shots of whiskey or between the fat thighs of a whore who makes you pay dearly. You come out of the brothel and set out again, and one day you end up putting a bullet in your head."

7

The train moves forward by fits and starts, its progress repeatedly interrupted, complicating Ito's task. On his lap lies the notebook. The thick, unmanageable paper slips through his fingers. It isn't only the train that has to race ahead, the words also have to, trying to recapture the past, the life that was, before imminent death. Ito Baraka is not trying to understand the things he and his comrades did, which side they were or were not on, whether he was a monster or a just man, how deep was the courage of some or the cowardice of others, no, he simply wants to roll the film and find each character in the posture that was his or hers, to grasp in its entirety and its precision a gesture, an image, an emotion, a laugh, a grimace. Bent over his page, he scribbles, crosses out, scratches.

———— ◆ ————

In our production of *Endgame*, Clov, the son, would witness the decline and fall of his blind, paralyzed master, Hamm. Clov would savour the gradual deterioration of Hamm, the master of the house—and of the country, in our fabulous creation, patriarch of the time of immobility. Clov, while playing the lackey and jumping at the slightest snap of the master's fingers, would run from behind the scenes to the front of the stage, where he would make us believe he actually had

power, the servant attending to every need of the master's dog, but
more and more threatening to leave the master. And the master would
finally die all alone behind the dark glasses of his blindness. Clov
would take wing like a seagull or a sinister, disturbing bat, and since
we were facing the sea, he could leave when he wanted to. And I must
say that at that time—and as always in tearjerker novels or movies—
sons would leave their families and go overseas, as I, too, did a few
years later. Clov would leave after checking that the birds had finished
eating Hamm's eyes and that the grandparents Nagg and Nell had finished rotting in their trashcans.

In our barrels, playing the grandparents Nagg and Nell, Sika and
I would portray the reality of the repression and corruption we were
living through, our old people thrown on the trash heap, shaking with
fever and dying on the doorsteps of their straw huts that would collapse in the monsoons, vanishing heaps of wicker and thatch, every
twig of which would float out to sea.

On the beach, the number of onlookers around our group was
swelling, we were close to winning our pretentious wager of present-
ing the immobility of the time as a heap of shit, with dying people
piling up, words stuck in rotting maws. After the rehearsals, once we
were out of the barrels, we would massage our joints on the beach,
and Sika and I would put away the barrels that held Nagg and Nell in
a warehouse in the big market facing the Atlantic. However, during
the last week of our rehearsals, Wali got sick with an infection, and we
decided, against his advice, not to do the play without him.

So we suspended our rehearsals, and we returned to our classes
with less enthusiasm and at the risk of forgetting our lines in the play.
On the airwaves, the same celebrations, commentaries, and testimoni-
als by the population describing all the favours bestowed by the single
party: peace, food self-sufficiency, authenticity, health for all by the
year 2000, complete nationalization of all mines and mineral deposits,
a green blue orange yellow red revolution. A green revolution because
our vitality and our salvation would come through a return to the land,
to authentically agrarian values. And in the darkness of the *maquis*,

the shadowy bars on the coast where we would go for a drink some evenings, things were said, such as that our prisons were full of dark, undesirable characters, that there was a militia that maintained order with, of course, the tools necessary to clean house if need be, and the forgetful earth, purged of the blood of torture, was once again virgin and ready to receive the seeds of the green revolution. And pending the year 2000 and health for all, they did not hesitate to beat up those who were resistant, and in the streets of the city the staging of parades and marches in support of the party and its green coffee cocoa banana cotton revolution continued, and I remember that prof who one day remarked, "If we have to support the party, it's because it's collapsing!"

It smelled like decline. Our character Hamm would collapse and tumble from his wheelchair under the mangroves from which mockingbird fledglings began to release their sticky droppings onto his bare skull in a volley of precise, coordinated farts. In the *maquis*, we analyzed the situation, speaking of the fault in the system and the impeccable order of the quagmire we were living in. The sturdy machine of power was going to start to sputter and cough. "If we have to support it, it's because it's breaking down!" "The green revolution," my father said pointedly, "is losing its stripes, its boots, its berets, its fatigues, and the honour of holding a leaden sky over our heads!" Another of our profs, I don't remember exactly who, would say, "There's a heaviness, put your hands up over your heads and you'll feel it." And we wanted to puncture the ball of heaviness above our heads with our impatient claws. In the bistros, people said the real revolution was still to come and that we would be its children.

Meanwhile, our chum Wali was consumed by illness, and this had become a much greater concern for us than any change of regime. Our group was overcome by a pervasive sadness. Wali was not recovering from his infection, and *Endgame* was beginning to look like ancient history. Those pithy bits of dialogue from Beckett were still in our memory and we didn't want to let go of them. We quite seriously called them "suppository phrases," to be shoved up the armoured assholes of the military thugs, the green ass of the revolution—the old one that had fucked us over—dry, without Vaseline, if you please. And when we met at Beno's place, we would read them again, just to touch their devastating beauty, especially Clov's lines when he was resisting the doddering Hamm or provoking him with his deceptively innocent questions. Little gems.

We started listing those gems, thinking of using them when the time came to put on the play, when we would display them in big letters on panels. However, that time was slow in coming, and we had forgotten many of the scenes and were going to have to start again from scratch. Wali was still weak, and because we didn't want to lose those words, we discussed how to make them available to passersby, to the crowds in the squares and markets, Beckett's shit scattered to the winds of the Gulf of Guinea. I recalled that, several months before, a book had circulated in our group that spoke of pieces of paper, leaflets placed on the doorsteps of houses in Warsaw, in Paris. I don't remember what book it was, or maybe it was just some article on resistance movements, the kind of thing we passed around at the time in the *maquis* and the halls of the university. We thought of Sony again, "They won't do anything to us!"

8

"They won't do anything to us!" I repeated to myself like a magic formula that would eradicate the heavy fear clinging to our skins, the shit that was impossible to expel, and as I've often done in times of doubt and anxiety, I thought of the only person who could make me forget that fear a little, or to be more precise, there was a chance that my wavering resolve would be strengthened, reinforced by my fight against that most extraordinary creature. I would have to confront that beast with bare hands and quaking heart, because although it would not be our first encounter, the beast still frightened me. Face to face with the creature, I had remained a timid kid struggling with a cruel stepmother with long teeth who was going to swallow him up, digest him and spit him out all soft after a terrible battle of bodies, with blows and wounds. But it was my therapy, and I knew that once the distance between us was eliminated, once I had broken the eternal ice of that inscrutable face and that tough flesh, once I found myself back in the vise of those rhinoceros thighs, I would have a sense of victory, and my feat would strip all substance from the fear. And I also knew that after the struggle, the Ogress, docile and maternal, would stroke my hair, my head nestled in her belly.

So one afternoon when we had no classes, I went to see her in the brothel in the Décon neighbourhood where she performed her duties. I arrived on the premises and told the manager I wanted to see the rhinoceros, Ma'ame Kili in person. We'd nicknamed her Kili for Kilimanjaro, to represent her huge body and volcanic nature. I remember the first time I saw her, which, to tell the truth, was my very first sexual experience. It was not with a beautiful ballerina at twilight on the seashore below the old wharf. No, it was with Ma'ame Kili, no less, in flesh and in volume. Wali had taken me there because he was convinced that the experience would loosen me up and make me more self-confident.

I arrived at the little room of the fat whore, a terrible fear running through my veins. I hesitated before knocking on the polished wooden door. It's not too late, I told myself, I can still turn back. I turned around and looked at Wali standing a few metres from the gate to hell and giving me a sign of encouragement. I knocked lightly on the door three times... nothing. One, two, three minutes passed... nothing. "Knock harder," whispered Wali, who had moved closer. I knocked again, a little more firmly, and a voice from behind the door thundered, "If that's how you announce yourself, I guess I'm going to be dealing with a wimp! So, are you coming in?"

And I went inside. She was lying on an iron bed in one corner of the room. Under her loose clothing, I could make out her huge body. I cursed Wali, that son of a bitch, why did you do this to me? I lowered my head and looked down, and she said, "It's not your head you have to lower, but your pants. Go on, do it!" I was furious, I had actually paid to be treated this way. I took off my clothes and she said, "Interesting, let's see what we can do with that. Are you coming?" And as she said it, she began to unbutton her dress. She didn't waste any time, she bared her massive bosom, a pair of breasts swollen with helium, horrible balloons from some ghastly party, and I wished those balloons would float up into the sky and I could grab hold of them and fly away, far from the trap I'd fallen into. Then I saw her belly, a huge, hideous, patchy tarpaulin with thousands of folds, a violent sea in constant motion, and it was clear that I was going to drown. A belly that spread out on the sheets like oil spilled on hot asphalt. Kili's limbs, ancient tree trunks hastily cut down in the sacred forest of

Bé, which was not far from the Décon neighbourhood and the brothel, tree trunks transported to the bedroom and attached to the rest of the body. But the most frightening thing was her tiny head, a ridiculous coconut in which shifty, suspicious eyes had been carved with a knife. Three hundred kilos of flesh assembled there for the pleasure or punishment of the thrill seekers she received in her ten-square-metre cloister. You'd think she must always have been there, it was impossible to imagine her dragging her cumbersome carcass on a journey.

Like the other times I had come to see her, I panicked when faced with the mountain. She said, "Here you are again! How long has it been, three months, six months?" She was already naked in the dark sheets. This time, the combat would end with my burial, and Wali would come to recover my body. Ma'ame Kili's belly overflowed, blocking the view I would have had of her immense pubic area and the vague beginning of her thighs. I lay down beside her, anxious. She rose on an elbow and ordered, "Mount!" She raised and opened her legs, and I found myself once again in her vise. Breathing heavily, I began to move one hand over that gigantic body. My plan was to conquer the giant, and then nothing could frighten me anymore. Ma'ame Kili was a wild, complex, untameable world that I had to possess, or at least besiege, I had to climb to the summit of the mountain and know that I had succeeded, and since my friends and I wanted to confront danger, I had to take her, that fortress of a woman, a Bastille in a brothel stinking of sweat and cheap detergent. It was 1990, and a black boy in the tropics was taking the Bastille. With my friends, I was going to topple the heads of our kings, proclaim Liberty, and finally change the world. Kili was the most frightening of creatures, and to approach her I would have to find resources of nerve I did not have. That was what we needed, nerve, and the brothel was not for well-behaved, well-brought-up children ready to jump at their parents' every command. Kili was my supreme act of defiance, my subversion, the rebellion of an altar boy trained and steeped in holy water by the Franciscans. I had just come out of the monastery to walk in the streets of discontent. I had to screw the hideous beast, and in the act my breathing became more and more normal, and that was the sign that the fear was finally gone, brutally expelled from my body with my cock's ejaculation into the belly of the Ogress. I could turn her this way and that in surprising mastery of her steep, dangerous geography. Her hard words and her rough movements were perhaps only a facade or part of a carefully concocted show. She became soft, docile, as if exhausted, and that was the sign that I had triumphed.

9

"Why didn't you ever go back to Africa?"
"I don't know. I could have."
"Is it nice there?"
"The sun there is always different, one day it warms you, the next day it kills you."
"It's not clear what you're saying. Why did you leave?"
"I didn't leave. I fled."
"What?"
"The shadows."
"You were afraid?"
"Yes."
"Of what?"
"Of another uprising. Of writing on the walls and going to hell again."
"Why did you write on the walls?"
"So people could read our anger in big letters. At least, we thought that was possible."
"And after you left, did you write on other walls?"
"No."
"Why not?"
"They weren't the same walls anymore. I shut myself up in a room to make books."

"With what? Your memories?"

"Words, a city, a house with a yard filled with noisy brats, people, pain, blood, lives, my mother and her block of ice that she carried in a pail to the middle of the market, my surveyor father and his ink drawings, and a prison cell with a dirt floor."

"A prison cell?"

"In a camp."

"Like a camp for a vacation?"

"Yes. A long vacation, locked in. In the company of a shadow, a friend, Koli Lem."

"Who's Koli Lem?"

"Someone who's gone now."

"Is he dead?"

"I don't know. I think so. He's dead."

"Where?"

"In detention."

"In the camp?"

"Yes."

"Is that why you wrote books?"

"Yes. That's what Koli had suggested. And I got caught up in it, one book, one play after another."

"Why?"

"It was a way to keep talking to someone."

"I don't understand anything you're saying."

"It'll come."

"And now you're sick."

"They're still trying to find a compatible donor for my leukemia."

"You refuse to go back to the hospital."

"It's too late."

"Why do you drink?"

"Good question."

"Why?"

"It gives you wings."

"And you fly?"

"No. You soar, you end up falling into the water with your burden of memories, you drown and you forget."

Ito Baraka remembers that conversation, the first one he had with his girlfriend Kimi Blue, his lover late in the game. He remembers it almost down to the last detail, impossible to forget the questions marked by a seeming naïveté, that childlike candour with which she takes things the rare times when she's not in need of a fix. Because Kimi does drugs. She's a beautiful junkie with deep eyes. Powder, for her, is a way to reach the clouds of forgetting. She injects herself with that nasty stuff and feels alive again. And it seems to Ito Baraka that Kimi dissolves more and more with every hit, she loses her substance as a living person and melts into her surroundings, between the walls and the furniture, flowing like a river that runs downhill, dead water disappearing in tiny trickles into the gravel and the voracious earth. Kimi, the one reason Ito Baraka wants the train to take him home fast. And when he gets back, Kimi, as usual, will scold him for getting drunk again.

It's true, Ito Baraka can't give up the bottle. In the evening, after another day spent hanging around in the city, he returns to his lair. He throws his bag down and collapses onto the bed, closes his eyes for an instant, opens them again and looks at the dead screen of the wall awash in darkness. He turns onto his side, one hand groping under the thick fabric of his coat for the flask, which he extracts from its hiding place. It's what he calls his midnight swig, the toast he drinks to the health of his fallen gods and ghosts. He shouts feverishly, "To your health, Bolívar! Go on, a good shot for you. To yours too, Vladimir Ilyich Ulyanov Lenin! To your health and an iron constitution, Amilcar Cabral! What has become of Guinea-Bissau? And Egypt, Nasser? What's the latest news? To your health, Fidel! Communism or death, long live Havana, its ruins and its half-starved people!" He drinks with those rebels of history, whose teeth chatter in the dark of the room, their jaws knocking together like those of puppets enraged at their irreversible state as powerless objects that can't do anything to change the decline of the world. Then he hugs the flask to his belly, rubs his eyes, and tries to sleep. The deep, cold night sucks him in. Then he feels a need to piss. He gets up and heads to the bathroom. He pees for a long time, his eyes half closed. He goes back to the bed, stumbles over his bag, loses his footing, falls over in the darkness and touches a cord, turning on a switch. The lamp on the bedside table lights up the room. He turns it off and lies down again in the fetal position, which gives him the feeling of having some control over his dying carcass, the feeling of being reborn in the tension of the muscles, the cracking of the bones and the dispersion, the explosion of his whole being. Heavy eyelids closed, he begins his negotiation with sleep, a hopelessly difficult task.

10

Ito Baraka runs a weary hand over his face. The passing of time has caused his silhouette to shrink and splinter. His face is a rectangle distorted by the premature wrinkles of suffering. He is forty-five years old, his skin sallow, his nose dwarfed by the Borsalino he has been wearing since he began to worry under the frequent dark clouds. An uncontrollable grimace twists his lips periodically, like a reaction to some inner jolt. In a few hours, he says to himself, he will be with Kimi Blue again. In the evening in the sheets, his hands will linger on her skin and the contours of her breasts, their disquieting fullness, the sheen of the nipples sculpted of the most precious wood.

The train jerks and pitches. The movement jostles Ito Baraka's hand, and he makes an unwanted line in the notebook. Ito Baraka doesn't know where he is. His face close to the window, he tries to peer into the night landscape. Beyond the snow-covered roof of the little station where they have stopped, raw nature, February and its evergreens with their frozen arms, the conical silhouettes barely trembling in the gusting wind. Ito shivers because of that other storm, the turmoil of the blood beneath his skin. He closes his eyes, opens them again, and picks up the notebook once more.

—— ◆ ——

With Wali sick, we suspended our rehearsals of *Endgame* and started thinking about making leaflets with bits of dialogue selected from the play. And there was that day when Sika showed up with the story she said her old father had told her, about the Fidelista students in Cuba during the revolution, who designed odd leaflets that instead of the usual slogans and political rants consisted of quotes from the poet José Martí, little phrases that sparked the interest of the people in the barrios of Havana better than pamphlets would have. Sika continued, "What do you think? What if we did the same thing and put our José Martí on bits of paper?" At first we didn't take her seriously. But she kept bringing up the subject, while I combed the library in vain trying to verify the story. And since we knew she wouldn't stop hounding us with her proposal, we finally said yes, if it worked for the young Cubans who loved José Martí, why wouldn't it work for us, too? And that's how we made our decision, essentially out of a crazy desire to identify with the Fidelistas, because for all our arrogance we had no confidence that we could change the course of things with our little pieces of paper. We knew the system was solid. This was an experiment that would either captivate us or quickly become boring. We didn't have any of José Martí's writings at hand, but we had our dog-eared Beckett.

And because, in any case, all the risks we considered in this mad undertaking led to a knot of fear in the belly—my visit to Ma'ame Kili at the brothel hadn't changed much—we took the plunge. We went to see Wali's cousin "Gueule de Bois"—"Hangover"—who lived in the Bé neighbourhood, which was an island of diehard rebels where the automatic rifles of the army were often heard. In an office in the back of his house, Gueule de Bois had a computer—a rare privilege at the time—which no one was allowed to touch. He wore Rasta dreadlocks and smoked profusely, in order, he said, to burn away the doubt and fear in him. And we spent entire nights there writing our weird leaflets.

We composed our leaflets, with Gueule de Bois at the computer while we chose our quotations. Sika had her copy of *Endgame* open on her knees, and before we plunged in, Gueule de Bois asked us for the hundredth time if we were ready. He warned us that if the wind turned violent, we would have to hang on tight. We couldn't begin to comprehend what we were risking. We looked at each other. Wali, still weak, had come to join us. Gueule de Bois smiled and said he'd never done "anything like this." I asked, "Like what?" He smiled again, "Leaflets like this." And we started putting together our fragments of dialogue. Today when I pick up *Endgame*, it amuses me to find the words with which we set out to make war on that nebulous enemy we called The System.

Our leaflets:

"How are your eyes?"
"Bad."
"How are your legs?"
"Bad."
"But you can move."
"Yes."
Impossible. Here, we
can't move.

The lines were Clov's and Hamm's, and the last part came from us.

> "I look at the wall."
> "The wall!" And what do you see
> on your wall? . . . Naked bodies?"
> "I see my light dying."
> The light is in us. Endgame for
> the sergeant and the boots!

Gueule de Bois burst out laughing, "It won't work! It's harmless poetry!" "You're wrong, Gueule de Bois, poetry has never been harmless," Sika replied.

> "What's happening, what's
> happening?"
> "Something is taking its
> course."
> The discontent, the spring is
> taking its course.

The eyes of the friends shone in the darkness. Gueule de Bois filled the air with smoke.

> "What's the weather like?"
> "As usual."
> "Look at the earth."
> "Look at the earth."
> Our land is consumed with stu-
> pidity and our earth is stained
> with blood.

We carried on, euphoric.

> "Grey... Grey! GRREY!"
> "Grey! Did I hear you say grey?"
> "Light black. From pole to pole"
> Black. In our heads, our neighbourhoods.

Very often, in the middle of the night, there would be a power outage. Gueule de Bois would light candles. The computer's battery allowed us to continue for two short hours.

> "Did you ever think of one thing?"
> "Never."
> "That here we're down in a hole."
> Our hole. It's possible to get out.

12

Ito Baraka has the feeling that the train, instead of carrying him forward, is taking him down under the ground, his suddenly heavy body plunged deep in a well, the very one that was in the middle of the yard at the first house he lived in with his parents. He again sees the bare earth around the well, the well itself, and the tall mango tree in what remained of the yard for the kids' games. He again sees the big pots of boiling water on the terracotta or wrought-iron charcoal stoves in front of each of the one- or two-room dwellings. The parents, who had nothing, would boil water all evening to make their children believe they would have a supper. And the pots would continue boiling until, overcome by fatigue, the kids would fall asleep on the laps of their sad, crushed mamas.

The train arrives in the Montreal station. There are no more connections to Ottawa. Ito Baraka heads outside to De La Gauchetière Street. His Quebec City hosts have reserved a room for him not far from the station in case he had to wait till morning for a train to Ottawa. At the hotel, the solitary receptionist at the desk makes short work of the formalities of registration. Once in the room, Ito takes a shower and lies down on the bed. He tries to reread the beginning of his story, but sets it aside. He grabs the remote control from the bedside table. Two or three hours flipping from channel to channel, a tour of a world that seems increasingly foreign to him as he withdraws from it. He gets up from the bed, thirsty. After serving himself from the minibar, he goes back and collapses once again. The features of the room become mixed up with those of a distant universe, and in his head, thousands of roads and faces come together.

Seven o'clock in the morning. Ito Baraka is saved from his foundering by the ringing of the telephone. He had asked for a wake-up call. Did he sleep? In the street, the cold chills him to the bone. At the station, he sits down on a bench in the main concourse. Employees are cleaning the tile floor of the huge building. Ito Baraka takes out his notebook again and tries to continue his story. He is advancing quickly despite the unavoidable slowness of his movements, the disease that is gradually stiffening his muscles and the joints of his fingers. His pen slips from his fingers again and falls at the foot of the bench. He has always written in notebooks. Early in their life together, Santou, his former companion, would type the texts on the computer in the straight, resigned posture of a secretary in some obscure suburban office. Ito Baraka bends over his page and goes back to scribbling.

———— ♦ ————

We huddled together in Gueule de Bois's little office and composed our leaflets until dawn, discussing the best terms, correcting, revising and in the end printing them out on the coloured paper that Gueule de Bois gave us for free. And when we asked him, "Why coloured paper?" the answer was obvious, our leaflets had to attract attention. And Gueule de Bois added, "For a change from grey." And the following nights we went out and distributed the leaflets, or to be precise, left them in specific places in the city—on the doorstep of the main post office, on the seats of university lecture halls, at intersections, on the beach, and in many other places where passersby couldn't miss them—at night, naturally, to reduce the risk of being spotted. We spent a whole week at it, and when we had left our packages untied in a given place, we would never go back there the next day. On the curbs, we would kneel as if to tie our shoes and put down the little squares of the leaflets, the knot of fear returning to our bellies when we saw car headlights coming towards us that could flush us out. At the university, it was easier, we would wait to be the last ones to leave the lecture hall after class and then distribute the papers. The next day, our classmates could talk of nothing else.

We continued distributing the leaflets in the dimly lit alleys of our city, carrying bags of the coloured papers slung across our shoulders. We had been at it for about a week when we got scared like never before. Because there was a story going around that more and more people were talking about. They were saying a group of young men, mainly students, had been arrested and transported to the office of the intelligence service on the outskirts of the city. There was little variation in the versions of the story, which meant that it must unquestionably be true. The boys had been putting out leaflets, and they were picked up in their homes in the middle of the night, roughed up, and taken to dark rooms, where information was wormed out of them with pliers and pincers, even if it meant ripping off their toenails, their nipples, their balls, and the rest. At sundown, the media confirmed the story, the black sheep were suspected of distributing subversive leaflets inciting, and I quote, "the army to revolt." Many people in the streets of the city knew what they were talking about, those pieces of printed paper where they read "things we were thinking quietly to ourselves, things that were burning our bellies," as Gueule de Bois would say later, "things that stabbed you in the stomach, and then you had no choice but to shit out the thing that was itching your guts." In the houses and the streets, they called the leaflets *adomenou*, which meant guts, those disgusting tubes inside the belly. The official communiqués stated that the purpose of the leaflets was to destabilize the regime and undermine the peace and security that had been established. They spoke of plots and a coup d'état, saying the *adomenou* were garbage, and any son of the nation who wanted to preserve the gains of the revolution had a duty to burn them. For the first time we were able to glimpse what the shit from our guts could represent, set out on sheets of paper.

And I imagined the sergeant with the Uzi trembling before those pieces of paper, the stinking tubes chasing him, trying to capture him, and him running, out of breath, in the corridors of his huge national palace with the *adomenou* on his tail, the guts that would tie him up and toss him into the lagoon, where he would be slowly swallowed up by the mud. In his bunker, the sergeant looks for a hiding place, he runs, stumbles, gets up, hides for a moment behind the frame of a huge photograph of his horrified face, slobbering on his colonial soldier's medals, won, as he has recounted, at Diên Biên Phu, in Alsace, and in Algeria.

In our *maquis*, we tried to imagine the lovely time the detainees must have had in the intelligence offices and we were scared stiff. A joking writer had said, "Speak up, they won't do anything to you!" Wali asked the question, "What are we risking?" We had thought we were the only ones distributing leaflets at night, and now we'd discovered that there was very likely a structure that was more organized and more serious than ours. It hadn't been a game for those boys, whose balls were undoubtedly being subjected to cruel caresses while we were talking.

Wali asked his question again: "What are we risking?" And the next day, we rushed to get rid of our remaining pink papers. I called Gueule de Bois's sister, and she told us in tears that he had been picked up the night of the roundup. Terror. A live flame burned my back and I recalled the inscrutable smile Gueule de Bois always wore. He must have been enjoying the all too lyrical quality of our leaflets, because there was nothing poetic about the shit from his own guts on pieces of paper. I cut short my phone conversation with his sister. My friends, in a circle around me in Beno's little room, were trembling like a person sick with malaria. We told Beno's father, who said sarcastically, "I could give you some quinine to calm your nerves, you impulsive little shit disturbers. But I can see only one thing to do, hide, and watch your step until the storm passes." For two weeks, we holed up with some colleagues of his and with an old priest who did not disapprove of our action, who said that it was bound to happen. Later we learned that there were about fifteen detainees, including our friend Gueule de Bois. It was a scorching August for us.

13

Aromas of coffee and fresh fruit surprise Ito Baraka on his bench. An old lady, who must also be waiting for a train, has come and sat beside him with her breakfast. Ito Baraka wonders in what morning market the old lady has bought her fruit. He remembers that, back home, the fruit merchants were the first ones to set up their stalls at Hanoukopé Market. He sees the market again, with the movie theatre in the middle. It was bounded by a lagoon that every evening sent down on people's heads an army of disciplined and lethally effective mosquitoes. There were open-air sewage ditches running alongside the houses like veins carrying bad blood under the skin of a stoic, dying man who doesn't give a damn. There were scrawny trees spreading their bare branches, beetles tickling the naked bums of the hordes of kids in front of the concessions with their bleached wood gates opening onto yards, each one with the indispensable well in the middle, the sole water supply for the tenants of the houses lined up on either side. And in a corner farther away, surrounded by a low, crudely built cinder-block wall, the sanitary facilities, two shower stalls on the greenish ground and a latrine, yes, a single one for the whole concession. So there was always a line of people waiting while you emptied yourself of all your frustrations, and sometimes someone pounding on the door to put pressure on you or clearing their throat to signal their painful presence and ask for a little compassion. Yes, that's the way it was, and Ito Baraka imagines it's still that way, the laterite dust and the smell of the gaping sewers hanging over everything like a sinister circus tent, the shine of tin roofs in the sun, the bars on the single window of the two-room apartment his parents rented. Bars, as if they were in prison, trapped in that working-class neighbourhood that at least wasn't in the slums of the outlying districts, bars that gave them a view of a striated, saturated sky. The sun beat down, making it unbearably hot in the houses, with their low roofs and no ceilings, and the tin nailed directly onto the palm-wood rafters scorched the skin.

That scene was where his mother would be, hawking ice water in the market. At the height of the tropical heat, that might bring in a few small coins. His mother among the wooden stalls and stands of a market along a railway line, "Ési, ési, de l'eau, de l'eau," a plastic pail hanging from her right hand, and in the pail, a big chunk of ice. At the public tap on the edge of the market, she would pour water over the ice and begin her round, "Ési, ési . . ."

His mother's dream was that Ito Baraka would get out of what she called their quagmire. He was not unhappy, but his mother, who had her own idea of happiness, had decided his destiny should be different. She thought that school, knowledge, would save him from the margins and give him a place at the centre of the world. That was also the credo hammered home daily by Baka the teacher at the Franciscan school where Ito Baraka began his quest for knowledge. "Learn reading, writing, and arithmetic, succeed, become an accomplished person!" Baka would repeat. Many years later Ito would say to himself that the issue wasn't mastery of numbers and letters, it was something else. The question to ask yourself was rather this one: "Of what night of the world are you the fruit? The one in which love, in the scent of a woman, gives you wings, or the one that keeps your eyes constantly fixed on nothingness, a hell long ago deserted by Eurydice and everything that has the face of tenderness? How, with what words, do you explain your night?" And it was to flee that confrontation with his hell of the night that Ito Baraka got into the habit of wandering the night streets, hanging around the streetlamps that push back the darkness. Alone or in the company of other insomniacs, he's a squatter on the streets of night under the light. He wanders aimlessly under the streetlamps, sensing in the sewers beneath his feet the hell populated by rats, and that's what he refuses to be, a rat crushed by the weight of the city and the centuries. Under a streetlight, he sits down on a bench with cold metal legs, turns the collar of his coat up, and closes his eyes. He closes his eyes and opens wide his depressed rat's ears, because, in spite of his refusal, that's what he is, a sinister, sad rat. He closes his eyes under the light and hopes for a miracle. The miracle of a trip through the air outside his complicated, tortured body. But he knows very well that rats don't fly.

The old lady sitting beside him in the station has finished her meal. She's wearing a dress of incredible whiteness. Ito Baraka likes white. It reminds him of the floor dusted with corn and millet flour at Abdul's mill on the corner of a street back home. It also reminds him of pagnes, the wraparounds worn tied around the waist by Voodoo priestesses doing their shopping in Hanoukopé Market. And white is the image of a miraculous peace, which soothes him.

So, to his relatives, Ito Baraka had to leave. And perhaps come back to them again one day, whether they were dead or survivors, palpable or fleeting shadows gathered in an airport lounge to welcome the revenant. His little cousins would be grown up, and his aunts, their mouths toothless and wrinkled in comical expressions, would demand kisses on their withered cheeks. If they hadn't croaked by then. Like his father, long since dead and buried. But Ito Baraka is one of those who don't go back. Poor wretches with dead eyes, frozen limbs, and backs plastered to a curb in Manhattan or Rome, their beggar's caps in their hands. For him, it will soon be the last act, the doctor confirmed it to him in his precise, methodical, rigorously impersonal voice: "Mr Baraka, let's say a few months at the most, but you never know. Above all, avoid tiring yourself out."

And now, he examines with a distant eye his life spent on the roads since that night in September twenty years ago when he left the country, the sober goodbye at the airport surrounded by his four brothers and sisters, who encouraged him with little pats on the back, pushing him into the Roman arena for a test of courage. A tear in the corner of his mother's eye, his father, after hugging him, standing back, apart from the group, already absent, as if he had decided to break the thread between himself and the others, to remove himself from the dim lights of the departure lounge. And one year later, Ito would get a phone call from an uncle: "The old man is dead." He didn't remember his father being old and sick, just the man with his body slightly bent from carrying his surveyor's tripod on worksites or bending over his maps and orders for house plans all day long.

14

The Ottawa train station, two hours later. His bag slung across his shoulders, Ito Baraka heads towards the bus platforms outside. Twenty minutes to wait for the 95 to the Rideau Centre, where he'll make his regular stop at the liquor vendor, who must know him well by now, who must be used to his quick grab for the bottle of Martinique rum, always the same one, like a little boy snatching a favourite toy. While he waits for the bus, Ito Baraka rereads what he scribbled on the ride from Montreal to Ottawa.

———— ◆ ————

I have quite a clear memory of that month of August when those students, the presumed leaflet makers, were arrested and locked up at the intelligence office. We spent the following days trying to assess the seriousness of their alleged actions and their consequences. Sika was constantly snivelling, Beno and Wali maintained the obstinate silence of hunted animals, and we spent the time while hiding out with the old priest trying to relearn our lines in *Endgame*. However, a few days after the media had announced the arrests, the majority of the detainees were released. Two of them were formally charged with distributing subversive leaflets, and rumour had it that they were not among those who had been released from the intelligence office. People who swore they had seen the released detainees said they were weakened, frail, mute, with empty eyes, as if they had spent their time in captivity drugged. I just remember that when we saw Gueule de Bois again, he appeared different, absent, bizarre. He didn't say much about what he'd experienced, but he told us a group of police officers had been very inventive with their torture techniques, coming up with all kinds of innovations. I think, rather, that the torturers' methods were traditional and brutal and refined. Gueule de Bois said nothing more about this, and a month later, the two accused were handed over to the city court for a first trial, which was quickly postponed because of a procedural error discovered by their lawyers.

The second trial took place two weeks later, in October, on a Friday morning. There was a crowd at the courthouse and dissent was in the air in the courtroom, which was packed with students, teachers, civil servants, merchants from the old market. The most enraged were brandishing slates denouncing this political trial. The women from the market were also there, they had distributed water to the crowd of onlookers who'd come to support the two accused. Outside, the human mass grew, and my father, who was surveying on a curb downtown, had to abandon his task and fold up his tripod, jostled and finally carried away by the tide.

My father would in spite of himself be immersed in history again that Friday when the echo of a chorus reached him from the courthouse. The crowd had begun to sing the forbidden former national anthem, which a lot of people had not forgotten, as would have been expected, since time had passed and a good part of the crowd around the courthouse had not known that song of fervent patriotism that the military had traded for a banal incantation calling on the people to reject troublemakers who undermined national unity. The crowd was convinced that the judges had been ordered to discipline the young miscreants, and everyone expected a speedy trial that would send the two rascals to the dungeons of the nation, where their parents would once a month bring them rotting fruits, since, as rumour had it, all fruits of the revolution were suspect. And my father, too, standing in the sun outside the courthouse, carried away by the general excitement, took up the old anthem. The electrified crowd, its volume increasing by the minute, was going to storm the courthouse and try to free the two accused.

The demonstrators pressed closer and closer around the courthouse, shouting and raising fists, placards, and rocks, and my father thought that at least at that particular time on that special Friday, fear had set sail across the stormy sea. Only the judges and the police were afraid. People said that was when the state prosecutor called for more police and soldiers. The crowd was now wild, and when the reinforcements arrived, they fired into the packed mass of people, emptying their clips into the forest of gleaming bare skin, reloading and firing again, opening breaches into the mass of flesh, and leaving rioters on the ground. The official media releases spoke of four dead. My father, with his tripod, found himself running away as fast as he could. The crowd scattered into the neighbourhoods, and there began a period of insurrection, pitched battles taking place in the streets between the police and the protestors. We joined the rioters in the heart of the city, where there were tires burning at the intersections, and later I learned that some police stations had been set on fire and so had the intelligence headquarters and some government vehicles, and I couldn't help thinking that it was a hell of a mess. Columns of fire rose at the intersections and young men, bare-chested, threw stones and Molotov cocktails at the army vehicles, something that had, of course, occurred at other times and places.

A springtime born of a few words printed on pieces of paper, and some people had been killed and others had disappeared. In the streets of insurrection, against a backdrop of rising smoke, some stones landed on the windshield of an army jeep. Behind the jeep were three other vehicles, paddy wagons. Men in fatigues jumped out and surrounded us. A girl who had thrown a last rock at them was shot in the knee. I had lost sight of Beno, Wali, Sika, and my cousin Sefa, who sometimes joined our group, and who very often was more caustic in his diatribes against the government than we were. The soldiers shoved us into the paddy wagons, and while we crossed the raging city, more projectiles landed on the vehicles. We were held all night in the courtyard of an army camp in the city outskirts, sitting in the sand with no clothes but our underpants, under the watchful eye of a Kalashnikov that frequently poked us in the neck. I was cold. And at dawn, they threw us some old clothes, loaded us into jeeps, and hastily blindfolded us. We were driven away, and I assumed they were not taking us home.

15

Once I'd gotten out of the military jeep, the guards took the blindfold off, and my eyes fixed on a grate in the middle of a long cement wall. The air smelled of bird shit and fresh dung from an unseen cow. After passing through the grate of that dreary entrance, we tramped through wet grass. That's my first memory of the camp, the smell of grass and earth wet from the morning rain, grass for about fifty metres before a barer area, more dirt than vegetation, with buildings on either side of the path we were following. And right away, along both sides, I saw the shine of barbed wire under a timid sun, its strands twisted and nailed to wooden stakes, its sharp knots discouraging any attempt to escape. But what would dissuade prisoners the most was not so much the wire and the sharp points as the armed guards sitting under the acacia trees along the central path, cigarettes dangling from their lips and rifles slung across their chests. I recall that one of them spat as we went by, a thick, heavy brown glob that landed in the middle of the path, and later I realized that he and the others must spend their time chewing kola nut, smoking, and drinking the ubiquitous millet beer out of small gourds. They were drunk and nervous, and we were afraid they could shoot at us at any moment, just to give their weapons some exercise.

I counted three of them on each side of the path, watching the prisoners without batting an eye. In the yard on our left were the older prisoners, about fifteen of them, I observed later. On the right, the younger ones, silent, resigned, barely turning their heads as we went by. I heard a sort of scream from the old people's side. In front of us, bushland, above which you could make out unfinished cement walls and tin roofs, two identical buildings that must have measured about fifty metres by twelve. I forgot to mention that there were fewer young prisoners than old ones, a dozen at most. Our guards shoved us from behind and we went around the two buildings to a less shaded area where there were some tiny structures of the same cement and tin, twelve cells set randomly on the bare earth, four smaller ones in back and eight others in front. We walked between them, along the corridors of an absurd topography. I was pushed by the shoulder towards the one furthest from civilization, and beyond it I could feel the wind and the bush. A bird flapped its wings violently and fled into the fields, and I barely had time to notice that the cells at the back had no windows when I found myself in the dark, and the metal door closed, heavy and creaking. The dirt floor was warm, and soon it would be baking in the sun.

My watch and my shoes had been confiscated in the jeep, and in any case there would have been no point in knowing the time, since time was going to stand still. I surveyed the cell, two metres by one, no more, and when I stood up straight, my head touched the burning tin of the roof. That's where I spent the first three days of my incarceration, in isolation, and I would later discover that this was a classic method used in detention facilities: isolate the prisoner and break his resistance. There was nothing special about this treatment, except that I had to make do with two square metres of living space. I lay down on the ground and immediately fell asleep. I slept for a few hours before the afternoon sun began to play tricks on me. The uneven surface of the dirt floor was imprinted on my ribs, and in the stifling heat, I realized I was thirsty. I turned onto my back and the overheated tin assailed my face, so back onto my side again, my knees bent against the cement wall, which had also heated up. I closed my eyes, trying to find sleep again, and I thought about our house, cool in the shade of a wild mammee tree. I thought about it, and I understood that I shouldn't do that anymore. I opened my eyes, my thirst still intense, and tried to swallow nonexistent saliva. I stretched my neck to try to get rid of the feeling of dryness. It was no use, and faced with the hopelessness of the situation, I panicked for the first time since my incarceration. I banged my forehead against the wall, but the unbearable longing was still there, and it didn't diminish until the next day. Many years later, when I read Kertész's *Fatelessness*, I had to agree with him that the first hours of thirst are the hardest. After that, it changes to a different sensation.

That heavy afternoon I remained lying down, holding my head in my hands, and after a period of time that I had difficulty estimating, there was a rustling sound against my cell. I started. Outside, a loud laugh, footsteps circling the cell two, three, four times, then stopping, the laugh again, silence, immediately followed by the sound of someone pissing on dead grass. I pictured the yellow liquid cascading onto the ground, and that had the effect of diminishing my thirst for a brief instant, as if the awareness of a source of water on the other side of my wall could satisfy me. The sound continued for several minutes, and I plugged my ears because it wasn't funny anymore and I could no longer find any consolation in it. It went on for a good quarter-hour, the long piss that must have come from a mythical giant, and later I understood that it was part of the program for new residents, the aperitif before the menu of torture.

And little by little, it was as if the water outside had put out the fire on the roof of my cell. It must have been dusk already. I tried to fall asleep again but was soon awakened by more laughter and shouts. In the bush, there were stamping and rustling sounds, and later I learned that this was the time of day when the guards could do whatever they wanted with the prisoners. In the high grass, they could shove anything they wanted into the bodies of those unfortunates, including themselves. It was before dinner, when they would serve us the inevitable maize porridge, hard as a rock and with no sauce, or if it was a special day, with a little bit of chili pepper. You had to behave yourself with the guards. The rape outside lasted a good hour, soon followed by a new silence and a song, I mean the racket of the mosquitoes that came to brighten our evenings. I slapped myself when the first one brushed my cheek, and as if I had offended the creature, the whole company of them came after me. I pulled the collar of my shirt tight, its sleeves seeming too short now, but I couldn't do much for a good part of my body. Strangely, night came quickly. I heard something like barking, and later, moans echoing. It was the time of day when game trapped by hunters on the savannah would die after a long agony, a paw torn off by the teeth of the trap. I shivered like a real weakling for a good part of the cold night, and I finally fell asleep.

I found myself in the middle of a desert, in a world of sand dunes that went on forever. The camp around me was swept away and my cell was becoming more and more isolated. Outside, the sun was drying up corpses that were lying on the ground, or it was liquefying them, the heads gradually melting, then the necks and shoulders, the sand swallowing the liquid as black and viscous as tar. I had a tiny window from which I could see this scene of the end of things, and I had no choice but to remain in my prison. To stick my nose out would mean running the foolish risk of liquefaction, and under my feet I heard the sound of that dirty water that runs in the bowels of cities and the movement of rats in the sewers. I was living in a world of rats. And that word would be the favourite insult of our guards. "You dirty rats!" they would yell time and time again.

16

In his head, Ito Baraka runs through the names of the revolutions of the current century and preceding ones. Revolutions with unforgettable nicknames: the Red, the Orange, the Carnation, the Arab, the French, the Castroist, the Quiet, the Pink. And the "pots and pans revolution" of the previous summer in Quebec, with kitchenware used as drums by the discontented students, whose sound and fury almost destroyed Ito Baraka's ears and his weary heart. Striking names and dramatic actions. There were people who carried out attacks, their bodies transformed into bombs blowing up the hearts of cities, those who occupied the streets and the big squares with war chants and clamour, those who shot or decapitated emperors and kings, those who, one day in the spring of 1989 in Beijing, stood up to fearsome tanks and the huge mouths of cannons, and those who bared their chests and their asses to protest idiocy, injustice, the clergy, corruption, and everything.

The 95 bus shows its chrome-trimmed red face. The driver stops and Ito Baraka takes the only free seat, in the back beside a homeless man who's drunk and enveloped in an aura of sewage and solitude. The man spits on the floor at their feet, blood. Two guys in the bus are dying—one doesn't care, and the other has a debt, a story to be told to a greasy, dog-eared notebook. Holding the notebook on his knees, Ito Baraka isn't bothered by the frequent stops of the bus, its bucking like a wild horse, or the conversation around him, or the other dying man spewing his bile. Ito writes, like an assiduous scribe or a resigned student trying to solve a complicated math problem.

———— ♦ ————

The day after I was incarcerated, I woke up at dawn with a horrible ache in my neck, although I had slept on my side. I tried to stand up and stretch my body. With the heat, my thirst came back, and my second day in my cell went by like the first one, with the sound of water on dead grass in the afternoon when the thirst became unbearable, rape in the fields before dinner, the guards' exquisite appetizer, the mosquitoes, the wild animals in the middle of the night, my hallucinations, another morning. I wasn't able to get up because I simply had no more strength, my vision was blurry, I couldn't crawl to the slop pail in the corner of the cell. I must have fallen asleep again after that, or maybe I fainted. I came to when I felt a burning light on me and someone pissed on my face after throwing me a piece of bread, which hit the dirt floor with a thunk.

Very soon, night returned, a third one, with the echoes and the torment of the animals on the savannah. I couldn't sleep because of a brutal backache. A fine rain pattered on the roof of the cell. I sat up and tried to bite into my piece of bread, the crust scraping against my teeth. I crushed the hard bread with my heel, took the powder in my palm and swallowed it. Later, I learned that they put treacherous little pebbles in the bread. I kept my eyes open in the dark and thought back to blind Hamm. Like him, I was in a kingdom of shadows and I wasn't wondering whether I was going to get out, and I recalled some of Hamm's lines, which I spoke out loud. Then, like Hamm, I made capricious demands of my servant, Clov, asking him to take me to the window to sense the sky and its smell and a boat in the distance raising anchor. I repeated the lines I remembered and I laughed very hard, I applauded myself, and at dawn, when the darkness in the cell became less dense, I had to abandon Hamm and his refuge from the eternal lazy night. Later, when it was hard to bear the screams and the scenes of torture, I would try to borrow from Hamm that night that takes away the sight of many things one doesn't want to see.

Hamm left and the cell door opened to a huge, heavy guy. He shouted, "Stand up!" and I just looked up at him because I couldn't get up. For an instant, I thought he was going to give me my dog or take me to the window to see the waves and the caravels leaving the harbour. He reached his big bear paw into the cell, grabbed me by the shirt collar and dragged me outside, my toes raking the ground and a carpet of thorns I had trouble getting rid of. He threw me into the yard with the young prisoners, a dozen withdrawn, taciturn boys who hardly glanced at me. The sun rose very quickly and I stayed lying in the yard. At breakfast, the guards threw us slices of boiled yam over the barbed wire. They must have been a good week old. I ate, it was better than the gravelly bread. We got a little water after that, in two pails filled to the brim, with two little gourds floating on top. I rushed over to them and drank half a pail, and I revived a little. I looked at the old prisoners in the other yard. Most of them were sitting, their backs bent, their heads lowered, reading some complicated message in the sand. They had very dry skin, like the bark of dead trees. An old woman in the flock was clutching the barbed wire, she was crying like a baby that had been taken from its mother, and her hands were bloody. An armed guard went over to her and gave her a slap that threw her into the dust, face down. Two more guards arrived, and they all went into the yard through one side that they had hastily unlocked. They ordered the old people to lie down with their faces to the ground, pulled down their pants and started whipping them with leather belts. Needless to say, the prisoners screamed like flayed animals. They had welts on their buttocks and strips of skin torn off. And the guards yelled, "Gang of sorcerers!"

And the next day, when the prisoners in my group became less silent, they explained to me that the old people were all accused of sorcery. Most of them came from surrounding villages where there had been unexplained deaths, disappearances of children, and too many sterile women, and they were blamed, they were surely the ones who had eaten the children, burned the fathers' souls, and messed up the women's wombs. There was evidence . . . they barely left their huts on the edge of the village, they were solitary, and dogs were afraid of them and didn't dare approach their homes. The village mutts, which could sniff out a sorcerer within a radius of ten kilometres, ran away from them, their tails between their legs, and tried to take refuge in the middle of the river. And that was the sign that they had identified a sorcerer. And it was said that the old people looked too satisfied when they met children, as if they were already tasting their blood, and that there was always a little more rain around their huts, filling their jars while the rest of the village barely received a few drops, only enough to wet the tips of their tongues. Sorcerers. And they were shut up in the camp where their bodies were subjected to an assortment of tortures designed to drive out the evil spirits and purify the soul. Water only once a week, a beating every three days, immobilization—meaning they had to stand for two full days like tree trunks in the landscape— as well as the sun torture.

The whipping that morning lasted a good quarter of an hour. The guards came back and sat down under the trees along the path, sat- isfied that they had done their duty, and helped themselves to millet beer. Then the one who was giving the orders and seemed to be the leader called someone over, and a little later, a rather thin, ageless man came with a broom and set about clearing the dead grass from the trail. Koli Lem.

Before I saw Koli again, I spent another week when my cell door would open in the middle of the night and the guards would drag me outside under the dark vault of midnight as in a ritual of some cult, a special initiation reserved for a chosen one. And with my head plunged in a bucket of dirty water or urine to simulate drowning, I kept thinking about Koli.

17

After our first encounter that day when Koli Lem was sweeping up dead leaves, I saw him again about ten days later. He was doing the same chore, staring vacantly like an automaton. I remember his spindly arms and their mechanical movements. A sweep to the left, a sweep to the right, as regular and precise as a rower, his neck straight and his eyes empty. And that same evening, I found myself with him in a cell bigger than the one I had occupied the preceding days, wider and with a window, if you please, with barbed wire on it, of course. I was to share my prison, because that was the custom. New arrivals, after a period of isolation, would be put with the older ones—not the sorcerers, but the other older prisoners, who, early in the morning, would go to work in the millet and yam fields near the camp. Because novices like me had to spend several weeks with our elders at the height of their decrepitude and madness. We had to live with those human wrecks so we would get a precise idea of what we, too, were going to become. I was supposed to share my evenings with Koli and watch him croak, as in a movie of what would be my own end.

Koli, my mentor in matters of death, was blind. I found that out the first evening when we were lying on our pallets and he asked, "What colour was the sun today?" A funny question. In fact, I didn't understand. He repeated, "What colour?" I answered, "As usual." He continued, "How?" Irritated, I retorted, "You saw it for yourself!" He smiled and said in a whisper, "My eyes are gone." Then he turned onto his side facing the wall, and five minutes later, I heard him snoring. I spent part of the night speculating that Koli Lem had probably not arrived in the camp blind. And that the same fate no doubt awaited me. When Koli was dead, I would be the new blind man of the place, the new puppet with spindly arms and a mechanical walk. But I wasn't sure he'd lost his sight in the camp. The next morning, I asked him, "How did you lose your sight?" He replied, "The sun." I didn't understand then. He left me alone and went off to do the guards' dishes and gather eggs in the henhouse. With his dead eyes, because he was used to it.

As for me, I was taken to a hut behind the young prisoners' yard. A bare room with a chair in the middle. I sat down as ordered by the guard, who already stank of beer. My hands were tied behind my back, and my feet bound with wire. Half an hour later, a tall, slender man arrived. He had big eyes and very black skin. He took a second chair from a dark corner and sat down facing my naked torso. He was smoking, like a torturer in a war or spy movie. He said, "How are you, my friend?" I replied that the wire was digging into my ankles. He replied, "That's to be expected. Let's talk. I know that many people in the capital think the movement around the courthouse and in the streets was spontaneous. However, we have information to the contrary. We know, for example, that there was manipulation. You were brainwashed by our political adversaries, those opportunists who don't have the balls to come out in the open. Now, tell me, weren't they the ones who sent you the money for the placards and banners? You didn't pay for all that with your miserable student stipends? We want to restore order, and to do that, we have to catch those jackals! Do you have names for me?" I shook my head, I had no names to give him. He smiled, looked down a moment, then straightened up, and wham! gave me a slap that landed me, along with the chair, on the rough floor. He placed his boot against my ribs and pressed down, and I whispered, "I don't know anyone, we just followed the crowd." He calmed down and said, "Very well, I'll give you the day to think about it."

I stayed in that position, tied to the chair overturned on the floor, for a good part of the day. Koli Lem came later to untie me. In the afternoon, I think. He gave me a piece of cassava to eat. Then I must have fallen asleep. I was awakened at dusk by shouting, the rapes had begun again in the bush. I learned later that it was mostly the sorcerers who were on the receiving end. It was necessary, the guards said, to get into their bodies through every hole. They used the expression "cleaning out the sorcerers." So that they let go of all the shit and evil spirits. A deadly ceremony. Bodies that were emptied and that consoled themselves by thinking their rotten waters could feed the earth and nourish hope.

After that first day of interrogation, I was taken back to our cell. Koli was waiting for me, lying on his back, hands behind his neck. He said, "Take the gourd under your pallet and drink." I did so, and he said, "And now, sleep." And, as was his habit, he very soon began to snore. The next day, the same program. In the evening, Koli asked if I could read to him. I replied that first we'd have to find a book. He lifted his mattress and I saw books. He smiled and explained that they were survivors from his former life as a teacher. And from that time on, we would live with characters other than the ones in our prison camp.

18

The bum sitting next to Ito Baraka in the bus also reminds him of a character in a novel, he's the perfect picture of a poor wretch. Ito again sees those characters who spent the evenings with him and Koli in their cell. Strange creatures of paper to whom he owes his survival. They had spirited confrontations, intense moments, skirmishes that they came out of shaken but alive. However, it was many years after the prison camp that he discovered the character who would mark him forever. Not one of those who inspire you to cling to life. Hero or shadow, that exhausted character with dangling arms, that painful spirit from the pen of Bohumil Hrabal: Hanta, in *Too Loud a Solitude*. Hanta alone in the hole that is his home, crushed under the weight of all the books he has saved from destruction, a romantic messiah-come-lately. Hanta, executioner of books and knowledge deemed subversive by the Czech regime, Hanta destroying the volumes in a compacter in which he himself will end up dying with his books. Ito Baraka considers that an end that is both tragic and beautiful, as the endings of novels can sometimes be, the chance Hanta had to choose the outcome of the story, with the hero plunging into the gaping maw of the compacter surrounded by Goethe, Shakespeare, Rousseau, Dante, like a patient in the hospital at the final moment when he must resign himself to throwing in the towel, with his wife, children, parents, friends, and colleagues around him.

Ito Baraka knows his girlfriend Kimi Blue will be there at the end beside his burdensome body, even though he wants to spare her that unnecessary torture. Yes, Hanta, because of the choice of his end, a semblance of nobility regained. Because, thinks Ito, back home, there are many who weren't able to choose their exit, cut down by a tropical fever or the whistling bullets of the republican army, dead on the seashore with a knife in the belly or burnt to a cinder at the wheel of a car or floating amid the garbage in the lagoon. He feels he is lucky that he can choose his own end. Like Hanta, he will write the last act as he wishes, although he has the impression that Kimi Blue will do everything she can to keep him on the stage.

Meanwhile, he wants time and the changing of the seasons to stop, and things to pause on Kimi Blue's skin, breasts, body while he continues to touch, to caress the oval face of that girl with her brown skin, high cheekbones, and almond-shaped black eyes and the surprisingly cool, deep voice that takes the time to polish each word. Kimi, who can display a serenity that reveals nothing of the junkie, and that is spoiled only when she begins to need a fix.

In the bus, the bum jostles Ito. The image of Kimi disappears, the contours of her body become hazy as though she no longer had breasts, and that thought is unbearable to Ito.

19

His obsession with breasts is an old story. It goes back to the time of the great glory of the single party back home, when breasts had a role to play in the revolutionary struggle against imperialism.

Ito remembers, at the peak of what the party called political animation, recruiters would come into the neighbourhoods looking for girls to instruct in patriotic dancing and singing. The girls would be taught to sing at the top of their lungs and wiggle their hips, to stamp their feet on the ground to trample the enemies of the revolution, to vibrate their whole bodies in rejection of neocolonialist projects, to shake their bosoms to show anyone jealous of the national awakening that the people were bursting with life, electrified, galvanized, ready to meet the challenges of the present and the future. In the municipal stadium, at the many nationalist festivals, there were choreographies of those busts in full bloom, with cannons firing red-hot cannonballs at the enemies of the nation, and the dancers' breasts jiggling. And since the girls were very young, barely out of their teens, they had breasts that were firm and hard and taut and that threatened to poke holes in their costumes. Their chests wet with sweat, their clothes would cling to their skin, revealing the arrogant beauty of their shining round breasts. Their arms open in the form of a cross, the girls would shake their bosoms, leap backward, and push their breasts forward, deadly grenades with the pins pulled, aiming at invisible targets.

And watching those shows, Ito Baraka had his first erections, just as the officials on the platform must have had, those respectable gentlemen fixated on the breasts, which they were ranking and sorting mentally according to their degree of firmness, deciding which girl, after the festivities, would sweeten their night. They would choose the most beautiful breasts to knead and nibble in their waterfront hotel rooms costing a small fortune.

And the day after the celebrations, the girls would come out of the hotels drained, their chests sore, their breasts crushed, their nipples munched on with champagne. The officials gave them gifts, large bills and jewelry, but since those gentlemen detested condoms, the girls would return to their shacks knocked up and with a nice assortment of diseases. And nine months later, there would be brats with hostile eyes in their arms suckling, brats bawling and draining the breasts of those little mothers, dozens of nursings a day, breasts that were beginning to point toward their navels, at half mast, already far from the days of glory and cannons. On their chests, unsightly bags drained by their pitiless offspring, the little mothers were turned into tropical cows nourishing the next generation, and no one, no lover in his right mind would want to touch those slackened, ruined breasts. And since the presumed culprits, all men of power, did not acknowledge the children, the girls had to get by one way or another. And when they scanned the horizon, they could see only one way, just one, to bring a little money into the house. So while the resigned grandmothers watched the kids, the girls went out to walk the street, offering their leftovers to anyone who wanted, their breasts decked out in provocative tops, and as they leaned over the car doors negotiating, the undecided clients could contemplate the drooping charms of these beauties of the night. The men would become stingy, no point paying a fortune for those crumpled bags, never suspecting that those breasts had been the best weapons of the anti-imperialist revolution.

And from sidewalk to sidewalk, the twilight of the breasts came very quickly, the girls worn out, wrinkled before their time, prematurely aged, sitting on the doorsteps of the houses, their busts now deflated, flat, their breasts flaccid, useless, covered with ridiculous wrappers or simply left uncovered, the old women, bare-chested in the hope that the wind might swell the dugs hanging under their chins like old socks. The wind didn't help, and the sun came to finish the job, pumping what was left of the blood from those hideous rags. It was not unusual to find those women dead and stiff in front of their huts, in a lovely illustration of the end of things, the end of life and of beauty. And there was nothing left to do but sing a requiem for those girls whose bodies, ten years earlier, had been so firm.

The reason Ito Baraka never tires of looking at Kimi Blue's breasts and watches over them is that he's afraid they, too, will begin to decline. But he's surprised to note that they remain firm as in youth, when so many things, follies and victories, are still possible. The implacable wheel of life has not yet passed over them. With those breasts, Kimi Blue remains alive, and that's the only ray of light that remains for Ito. So, every day, he asks his girlfriend not to spoil her breasts, he doesn't want to see her looking like those dried-up women he saw in the streets of his youth, laid low by bad times, like those sorcerers in the camp where he was detained. He clings to Kimi's breasts because they alone still connect him to life, to madness, and to blind hope.

20

Ito Baraka gets off the 95 bus at the Rideau Centre, the commercial heart of the city of Ottawa, and heads towards the wine and spirits store where he's a regular. His gaze drifts over the store windows, his right hand gripping the escalator handrail. He steps into the shop, grabs his rum from the shelf, pays at the cash, and stuffs the wrapped bottle into his bag. He reflects that if the government, by some absurd decree, were to put all spirits under lock and key, a lot of budding poets would kill themselves after trying in vain to pull some timeless masterpiece from the bottoms of their empty glasses. He comes out of the shopping centre and heads towards the stop for the buses to Hull, on the other side of Rideau Street. The rising February sun provides a semblance of warmth on his head, and he's thirsty. Before taking his last bus, he goes into the Chapters bookstore, where a front corner has been turned into a café. He orders a coffee and sits down at a table facing the street. He's served his coffee, he takes a sip, looks up, and can't fail to observe that he has just missed his bus. He'll take the next one. On his lap, his bag suddenly feels very heavy. He takes out the notebook and lays it on the table. The pen, like the flask, is in one of his inside pockets. He takes it out and finds Koli Lem where he had left him.

— ◆ —

Before he was imprisoned, Koli Lem was a teacher in a village in the same region where the camp was located. He taught the last year before high school. Thirty years teaching algebra, ethics, history and geography, calculus, civics, and patriotic songs, according to the curriculum devised by the party. He had to follow that idiotic curriculum. And often he had to take the children to the town five kilometres from the village to form an honour guard for a prominent guest the country had a duty to welcome with appropriate pomp and ceremony. Four hours standing along a road in the scorching heat, and when you least expected it, the guest's cortege would speed by. And the surprised crowd could only applaud the disappearing Mercedes and its illustrious passengers. Four hours in the sun or rain for that farce. Then again, you couldn't say most of the children were unhappy about it. It was a chance to skip school. Jeeps followed the cortege to protect the behinds of the guests and keep an eye on the crowd of school children. You never knew, some little smart aleck armed to the teeth could be hiding among the young people to take a shot at the asses of the distinguished guests.

And once back in class, the kids were much too pooped to take in the teacher's lessons. They were no longer receptive, they even dozed off, and in the evening some of them would have to go to the courtyard of a village chief for rehearsals of dances and songs for the political animation, when they would shake to the fervent melodies of the revolution, ready to grace the thousands of celebrations on the calendar of the nation.

Then came that week when yet another distinguished guest was passing through the region. Koli Lem got ready to act. He bought some castor oil at the only pharmacy in the area, ten kilometres from the village. Castor oil, and all night long, he wondered if he would go through with it. He barely slept. The children were supposed to set off around ten o'clock the next morning to form an honour guard for the despot. Koli Lem couldn't stand to watch them go through that again, and in the middle of his restless night, he dreamed that the Revolution, a lady in black holding a pitchfork, was breaking down the doors of the huts in the village and gobbling up the little kids, who didn't have the tough skin of the older people, indifferent now to the ravages of time. The lady with the pitchfork snapped them up with a flick of her tongue, her mouth bloody, and moved determinedly toward Koli's hut at the edge of the village. She plunged the pitchfork into the door and sent it flying. She burped, and Koli woke up. He went and showered behind his hut to clear his head, and at dawn, he made his decision. He would do it.

That morning in class, he told the children he was going to give them some medicine that would help them digest their food, so that they would feel less heavy and would better learn their lessons and memorize all those calculus formulas for the year-end exams that were fast approaching. And because they, of course, all wanted to pass, they didn't need much persuasion. They lined up in front of Koli, and each in turn gulped down a good tablespoonful of his oil. They made faces. It wasn't easy to swallow that disgusting grease. They sat down again and wiped their lips with the backs of their hands, and instead of the usual dictation, Koli Lem talked to them about his old dream. He confessed that when he was their age, he had wanted to be a pilot, and the cleverest of his little charges asked, "Like Saint-Exupéry?"

A girl in the classroom coughed and put up her hand, "Mr Koli, can I go to the toilet?" Without waiting for his permission, she dashed off to the lavatory. A minute later, the same problem occurred with another student, who didn't even have time to raise a finger, and another, and so on. The students were lined up at the lavatory, fighting to hold in the boiling broth in their bellies that was trying to get out. They stamped the ground impatiently, jostling to be first as soon as one of the three stalls freed up. Koli went to see the principal and told him that his children had caught some virus or bacteria and they couldn't stop . . . The principal came out of his office and saw the crowd in front of the lavatory. He said, "This is serious, I'm evacuating the school and sending the other classes out to the honour guard right away. You stay here with these poor kids." Koli replied that that was the best thing to do. This was at nine o'clock, and a quarter-hour later, he was all alone with his charges, who continued their ballet between the classroom and the toilets, emptying themselves more and more with each trip.

Around one in the afternoon, the fury of the waters in the children's guts began to calm, and Koli said they had gotten rid of the stagnant waters inside them that were rotting their bellies and heads. They didn't seem to understand, but by about four o'clock, they'd all stopped running to the toilets.

The day after that memorable event, the principal summoned Koli. He told him he had questioned some of the children. He had to make his report to the school inspector. A week later, he sent the report, and the inspector, a devoted servant of the party, did not take long to make the connection between the mysterious epidemic and the outing planned for the honour guard that day. One morning in September 1984, two men in fatigues came looking for Koli Lem at the school. A cruel, burning sun was shining.

21

The sun. At this point in his story, Ito Baraka stops writing and studies the street scene in front of him. The street and the anonymous crowd. A scene comes back to him of a seashore that could have been Lomé, Cape Coast, Port Said, or Dakar. But it isn't Lomé or any city on that coast where he grew up. We are somewhere in Algeria. The Arab, with his knife, is threatening Meursault. The reflection from the blade hurts Meursault's eyes, and to stop the pain, he shoots the man. And in court, Meursault, in Camus's *L'Étranger*, to show his contempt for the world, says he killed him "because of the sun."

During his teenage years in the alleys back home, Ito Baraka always wondered, "How can a person die because of the sun?" However, little by little, he added up the children and the old people and the more vigorous ones who had died trying to cope under the sun, added up all those indifferent skies under which the bullets whistling from the Kalashnikovs of the people's army would turn you into a sieve, or a bazooka would rip off a shoulder with the arm still holding a begging bowl. The sun, that ogre that eventually burned up fruits and memory. He would read that later in something by a Cuban poet. He hasn't forgotten, back home when the wily sky refused them rain, the sun burned the earth and the shoots of the beans and peanuts in the little field behind their house, and the ice melted in his mother's pail in Hanoukopé Market and the water that had become tepid could not slake thirst.

Koli Lem didn't like the sun either. He had a list of arguments showing the sun was to blame for the rotten luck and degradation of most of his kind, their tragedy. There was something seductive in the biblical clarity with which Koli made the link between the rough, chapped, prematurely furrowed faces of the prisoners in their camp and the merciless sun over their heads. However, Ito Baraka knew that his friend only half-believed that. You couldn't attribute everything to the sun. Koli didn't really believe it, as Ito could read in his friend's half-smile and ironic tone, the attitude of one who, after giving up on finding the cause of everything that has gone wrong around him, tries to provoke a reaction from the person he's talking to, who he believes could help him see things in a new light where he hadn't been able to discover any logic or explanation for their disaster, their dark night. And it must be said that Ito had never really contradicted his friend's attempts to shed light on the causes of their misfortune and solve the complicated equation of their tropical tragedy. The most important thing for Ito was that Koli should continue to fill their cell with his low, slightly rusty voice, with his urgent need to pour himself out. There was a tacit agreement between them, roles that they had naturally taken on. Koli Lem possessed the words of a fallen oracle and Ito Baraka—who at that time had limited experience of the treachery of life—had only to follow him.

And in the hope of making Ito loathe that nasty sun, Koli Lem told him the story of how, in 1884, a German explorer, Gustav Nachtigal, landed on the coast of the country and was welcomed by the locals, though they were suspicious at first. And very quickly, he signed a protectorate treaty with King Mlapa III of Togoville, and the country was entrusted to the Prussians, who soon had it surveyed from one end to the other. The warriors in the North, the Konkomba and the Chokosi, resisted fiercely for a time before laying down their arms, their archers vanquished, and the Germans burned their bows and arrows. And soon there were niggers lined up on both sides of a path that, little by little, would be made wider by their picks, the whips burning their dark backs, the railway taking shape, that line of metal that would cross a good part of the country, from the coast to the village of Blitta, the niggers digging the earth, lined up along the route, and hauling the ties and iron rails with their bare arms. And the Germans, helmets clamped on their heads, hitting and beating, "Raus, schnell!" "The colonists had their heads covered but our heads were bare, exposed, and that's how the sun gradually ate away our brains and our will," said Koli, "and we became docile, helpful little lambs of the good Lord. And in 1919, when Germany lost the war, the hand holding the crop became English, 'Go on! Move your lazy arses!' and later French, 'Allez, you bunch of lazy baboons, get a move on!'" We had thought they would supply us with ridiculous straw hats to cover our nappy heads, but nothing. And the sun continued to soften us, and you understand," continued Koli, "why I can't love the sun. Why I'm fine where I am in my darkness."

22

Outside, a girl wearing headphones prances along the curb. Ito Baraka likes to imagine the rhythm she's moving to. A few days ago, he had an idea, to take Kimi Blue dancing. But obviously he can't. Dancing, nostalgia, what back home was called a *bal poussière*, a dance in the dust. At night, in the lighted yard of a concession, between a mango tree and a table holding a cassette player. The *ambianceur*, the old version of a DJ, would play the music. And all those students, in a daze, would boogie all night until dawn in the tropical city, at a time when there wasn't yet a curfew, when the first love, the first breast stroked under a flowered dress, as Ito would read in a poet from Fez, felt like it would be the last. Love born in the night of bodies that touched and electrified each other, when the dance steps raised dust from the dance floor, which was rarely cement. Here in this distant north, there's none of that red dust with its hot smell that stuck in your throat and on your clothes. Ito Baraka would have liked to give Kimi a dance full of dust and the trembling of nervous thighs that end up opening onto that humid night in violent coitus.

That was what they did there, that was how Ito would sometimes enjoy himself with his friends in their house in the suburbs. Have things changed since? He knows in any case that his parents' house has begun to look like a ruin. The last time he called home, he got his cousin Sefa, who told him that the house was no longer what it

had been. Part of the fence had collapsed after the last rains, expos-
ing the structure to invasion by petty thieves. The walls of the building had begun to explode, cracks zigzagging up from the foundation,
making their way between the bricks they revealed, their threadlike
patterns reaching right up the wall to the reinforced concrete lintels
above the doors and windows, which stopped the upward progres-
sion of the disaster. But then the cracks started again, attacking the
roof. The floors of what remained of the bedrooms were also cracked,
and the windows were exposed to the winds, having long ago lost the
ridiculous plastic mesh that protected them from voracious little creatures and the debris and dust from the weather that was getting worse
and worse. The hallway door that had led to the backyard—where
they used to dance—no longer existed, and some angry, undisciplined
bats had invaded the premises and made their nests under the roof,
between the rafters. And the sheet metal that served as an awning
over the terrace in the front was now hanging dangerously to one side,
where the teak column had been ravaged at the base by termites. Not
sure you could still go to a dance there.

Ito Baraka sees the bus coming from his seat in the café facing the
street. He hurries outside. His notebook under his arm and his bag
thrown carelessly over his shoulder, he climbs into the vehicle, which
immediately pulls away, as if the impatient driver had only been waiting for him to get moving again.

23

The bus advances through the heart of the city. Ito Baraka has trouble believing that twenty years have gone by since that dull day in June when he arrived in Quebec, thanks to a writing grant, and took a bus straight to Hull, because an old buddy he had gone to university with in the Gulf of Guinea lived there. The patron who had bestowed the grant had continued to support him for months after the end of his contract, because Ito was curious about this northern land and had decided not to return to Africa immediately. Five years after setting foot in this country, in a park on the shores of a waterway where ducks were shaking water off their backs, he met Santou, who had come there to find a bit of the atmosphere of her native island in the Caribbean.

Six months after they met, he moved in with Santou, because he sensed in her something like a reckless trust in life that she refused to question too much. Santou: smiles, songs, and a beaming face, living in the present without asking for anything more. And Ito thought that a little bit of that childlike joy might pull him out of the tunnel that his own life had become. The first months of their life together seemed to bring the promised peace. At night, he would lay his head on her generous bosom in that narrow space of flesh and velvet between her breasts, he would close his eyes, and he'd wake up surprised at having slept, no longer feeling his own body like a weight in the sheets.

After six months of living together, they had begun to argue over trivialities or because, in reality, something, some indefinable note, was not right in their relationship. Obviously, it was he, Ito, who was not right. Santou wanted a child, while he was convinced that they were fine as they were, he was fine with his head buried in the saving sweetness of his girlfriend's skin. Why have a child? he would repeat. A kid he could only give what he called a legacy of anxiety?

They lived in the apartment, the burrow, that Ito has kept to the present day, in the basement of one of those run-down buildings in Old Hull. To make ends meet, he gave French classes to immigrants from Yunnan, Chile, Ukraine, and Libya in Ottawa and Hull. It wasn't literature, that bourgeois lyricism that allowed him sometimes in his basement to imagine he had the reflexes of an aristocrat while exercising his plebeian lucidity. He was supposed to teach them what was called a second language, the basics and the exercises needed for boring everyday conversations. He tried stoically to devote what he could of energy and enthusiasm to it, using textbooks and cassettes on which rigorously professional monotonous voices carefully articulated the words, and he issued a litany of instructions to his aging students, whose dentures fractured the syntax.

While he became more and more weary, in his head was an unfinished scene in the manuscript of a play, a hypothetical situation in which he had left his characters in the middle of the night to finally sleep for a couple of hours beside a sulky Santou. He would get home about six o'clock, have a bite, and sit by himself in a corner of the living room, joining his characters where he had left them in the early morning. Santou would stand at the window carrying on a dialogue with the deserted street. But in the middle of the night, a strange feeling of guilt would come over Ito Baraka, he would get up and go find his companion in bed sleeping restlessly, her dry lips murmuring a chant of depression. Under the sheets, he would run his hands over her body, tense like that of an embittered nun, and after their mechanical lovemaking, his face turned to the mildewed ceiling, he would understand that they were not in love. They had simply tried to unite their solitudes. There was no longer anything of the passion or the candid sweetness of the beginning of their story.

However, at the end of their first year of conjugal partnership, Santou got pregnant. Warily, Ito Baraka began watching the development of his companion's belly. When he came back from his classes, he would pass a curious hand over it, and Santou would smile, the child was going to close the gulf between them, transform the geometry of love. During this propitious pregnancy, Ito worked compulsively and finished two plays, which never found a publisher. And Santou began to complain, "You have to get a move on, my friend, we're not going to raise the child in this hole. Finish your thesis, find a job at the university, and you won't be so bored any more. Make an effort, my friend!"

And the child was born in the hospital in Hull on a clear night when his father was unable to hide his uneasiness. They returned to the basement and Ito went back to his hermit's life, not much disturbed by the inconvenient bawling of the newborn, nor by Santou's exasperated shouting over it, "We're not going to rot in this basement! You're trying to bury us alive, Ito. I don't want this! If I didn't have to look after the kid, do you think I'd be hanging around here all day long? You've lost your enthusiasm for your thesis, so do something else, look for a real job, become a civil servant, and you'll write when you have the money to buy yourself some time, because you're using our time to make up stories that are of no interest to anyone, and that's not what we need right now. It's money, my friend, to be brutally frank!" And one evening, she became even more bossy, and gave him what sounded like an ultimatum, "I won't stay with you this way for long, dear friend, I want to breathe fresh air, not the mildew and stale air of this hole! I want a real house for the kid! Don't you find that he coughs a lot? Because of the damp in this place and a crazy father bent over a rickety table scribbling page after page. A house for our son isn't too much to ask! And if you could look after him, I'd go out and hustle, but no, *monsieur* has no time, he's even cut down on his class hours so he can devote his precious life to scribbling, swearing, tearing off the page and throwing it in the wastebasket, and here we go again, scribbling, crossing out, screwing up. I've had it, Ito Baraka! We have to get out of here! I want a home, a properly heated apartment where we won't have to wear heavy sweaters and slippers all the time, a real kitchen, and furniture, not these shabby pieces of wood and leather we got for fifty bucks at Emmaus, and faucets that don't drip, and a bed, not this mattress on a box spring that squeaks the rare times you screw me, and you think it's me coming!"

Ito Baraka kept his cool and conceded that she was right. He added that as soon as he finished the play he was working on, he would make some changes. And she continued, vehement, "How many times have you promised me that? How many?" Then Ito got annoyed, and he called her materialistic, saying she put too much weight on things that shouldn't matter, and she said, "You're wearing me out. What doesn't matter, what's superfluous in the life we're leading? I should have realized you're a lost soul, one of those lunatics with a terrible curse over them, I've learned that it's not just an idea or concept, you really are a *poète maudit*, the proof is that no one understands what you're doing, and when the publishers send back your manuscripts, what do they say? 'Sir, in spite of the undeniable qualities of your writing, it is difficult to enter your world.' I should have suspected it, when I met you, you were reading Verlaine for the tenth time and you were talking about leaving for Ethiopia, for Harar, to follow in Rimbaud's footsteps. And when you came to this country, you rushed to buy all the Nelligan books you could find, and the rare times when we manage to copulate, Nelligan, Baudelaire, Artaud, and Vigny are peering at us from your bedside table, your arm knocks over the books, they scatter on the carpet, and your dead writers cough because those voyeurs want us to get it on! I can't take it anymore Ito, get a grip and let us live!"

24

Ito Baraka returns to his burrow with its damp, silent walls. He drops heavily onto his couch as if he's undergone an endurance test, he's a marathon runner whose body snaps at the finish line with a crack, like dead wood assaulted by the wind. And because, soon, the dead wood will be buried in earth and oblivion, Ito Baraka amuses himself by giving it a final task, so that his body is useful for something before the collapse, he amuses himself imagining an action, a remarkable feat of which his body will be the site. He could, he thinks, do himself in in some luminous action, an explosion followed by sparks. Or he could simply immolate himself in the middle of the city in front of the buildings where the politicians work, with a sign hanging around his neck urging the government not to forget poets, mad people, outsiders, or Kimi Blue and the junkies on the margins of our great story of progress and victory. That way, Ito Baraka's body could be useful for something, could set the tone of the revolution of the beggars and others shunned by our society, why not? But he knows, as a madman once said, you very often end up being swallowed up by your own revolution. The fire you've lit, through a cynical whim of the wind, turns against you, it pursues you and manages to catch you and burn your belly, your face, or your ass. Then Ito Baraka smiles, it certainly wouldn't be worth it to immolate himself. Or maybe it would. And if he did, what would happen? He'd mess up his spectacular suicide and there he'd be, disfigured, his face a repulsive ball of tattered flesh, smooth as the skin of a drum in some places, crumpled in others, a surgeon with his scalpels would do his best to give him back a human appearance, he would end up with, in place of his ears and nose, the bizarre orifices of some prehistoric animal, with more holes on the squashed potato his head would have become, and the rest of his body, don't even talk about it, one huge scar with folds and red blotches and furrows. His burned toes would resemble those of a leper forgotten in front of his hut in the back country in Mozambique, his belly a hideous patchwork of various mismatched tissues.

And burned like that and cut off from the world, he would be able to start his revolution again, as revenge for the past in the country where everything had fallen to pieces, as in Hervé Bazin's book about an arsonist who, at night, sets fire to houses to take out his frustration and rage, sets fire to everything that to him represents and promotes injustice.

25

On the sofa, Ito Baraka feels the tips of his fingers hardening. He's cold. Ice creeps insidiously under his skin. He shivers and beats his arms. Outside, night is falling. Ito Baraka stares at the latest pages he's written in the notebook. Perhaps the last ones. It is becoming more and more difficult for him to go on. Grimacing, he walks to the bedroom and comes back with a thick blanket over his shoulders. He hobbles to the window, not a living soul outside, the streets deserted and silent. To fill the silence in the apartment, he invents a song, couplets carried by a chorus of birds and agitated clowns.

The cold seems willing to give his fingers a little respite and they regain a semblance of mobility. Ito Baraka goes back to the sofa. The notebook on his lap, he grabs his pen and opens the bottle of rum he had set down at his feet. He drinks. On his tongue, a bitter taste. The alcohol eases the fire of the blood in his veins, which are warm now. Ito immerses himself in his half-full glass so as not to feel the weight of his worn-out muscles and bones and the knots in his joints. He tries to regain the illusion of freedom in his movements. His nervous fingers grip the pen and he continues his story.

———— ◆ ————

In the evening, "at home" in our cell, Koli would take a book out from underneath the pallet and hand it to me. In the middle of the night, the guards were asleep, knocked out by alcohol. There were only two sentries at the entrance, and because they couldn't see into our cell in the thickets, Koli could take out the oil lamp he had gotten from the kitchen and strike a match in the darkness. I would open the book at the turned-down page that served as a bookmark and we would continue our story where we had left off.

Koli had always had those books. In his hut in the village. After years as a prisoner, he was granted the right to a few visits annually. And when his nephew brought him the books he asked for, his jailers said nothing, the head guard just smiled, not seeing what Koli could do with books since his eyes were dead. And in fact, in the first weeks, before I became his cellmate, he spent his time stroking the covers of those volumes, which the nephew had chosen mainly for their large size. The nephew had put in each book something that would permit Koli to recognize it, such as a match, a square of cardboard, or a feather, and when it was a book Koli had already read, his fingers would go back and forth in the pages as he tried to rediscover the characters, an activity he quite seriously called worship. Together we read Bulgakov, with the meeting of the Master and Margarita, and the cat that jumps up and hangs on to the back of the tramcar; García Márquez, *One Hundred Years of Solitude*, with the unforgettable passage about the large underpants Úrsula Iguarán wore to protect her virginity; Chinua Achebe, *Things Fall Apart*, with the terrible scene of the sacrifice of the child Ikemefuna; and many other books, such as *Les Misérables, The Sound and the Fury, The Tin Drum, Hopscotch, Ulysses, Masters of the Dew*. And when I myself started writing, creating plays of my own, those books, characters, and worlds continued to haunt me. What I have written, I owe to Koli Lem and our evenings in our cell, our conspiratorial closeness within our four walls and our frustration when there was no oil left in the lamp and we couldn't continue our reading of a Saramago.

However, we didn't have all that many books, a couple of dozen at most, and because his nephew, for some obscure reason, no longer came to visit Koli, we very quickly exhausted our supply. We even repeated a few titles. We began to find our evenings long and hopeless, but despite that, I must say we were able to hold out during the day with all its bullying because in the evening we had an appointment around a Nabokov.

26

Then the day came when I underwent that interrogation, the last one, the one when I sold out my friends. It was early in the morning, I was barely awake and I almost didn't feel the huge arms that pushed me towards the confession room. The interrogator was waiting for me, his hands folded on a white wooden table, a new element in the generally spare decor. The cigarette he had started smoking was resting against the edge of a metal ashtray, a detail I saw better once the mists of dawn had faded. I was sat down on a chair facing the man, who had the elegant manners of a pretentious aristocrat. I wasn't shackled, and the guards left us alone, closing the door behind them. The man, instead of looking directly at me as he was quite capable of doing, gazed up at the ceiling beams and said softly, "You stated that you did not belong to any organized group. Well, I can tell you I have obtained information to the contrary." I trembled and tried to regain control by thinking of the exact words of Koli, who had warned me, "Be careful. Very often, those scoundrels will say things that are false in order to find out the truth. Stay calm, and never contradict yourself!"

After his introductory words, the man took his time finishing his cigarette. Then, from a small box at his feet, he took out a pair of pliers, which he laid on the table. Several prisoners had told me that the pliers meant things were getting complicated and you shouldn't continue to toy with the nerves of the torturer. It was best to give him any old story to avoid getting your fingernails torn out. The man continued, "The pliers are made for pulling nails from boards. Don't make me use them for something else. Tell me about your friends. I'm asking you to confirm what I already know. What were you planning and who manipulated you?" In spite of Koli's warning, it was hard to keep believing the guy was bluffing, and besides, my friend had forgotten to mention the pliers and other instruments in the box. And I recalled something another prisoner had whispered to me, "That devil doesn't leave you alone until you've confessed. To him, it's obvious we were all involved in a conspiracy against the authorities." I glimpsed the possibility of not having to come back before the interrogator and I tried to make my aims seem innocuous.

"I'm not part of any organization. Like all students, I had my group of friends."

"You had. Why are you speaking in the past tense? Aren't they your friends anymore?"

"Now I'm here."

"But does that change the fact that they're your friends?"

"Uh, no . . . "

"Very well. How many were you in your group?"

"Four or five."

"Be more precise. Unless there's someone you're hesitating to count as belonging to your circle? Why is that?"

"No, no one. Four. There are four of us."

"Who's the fifth person?"

"A cousin who sometimes joined our group."

"His name?"

"He didn't do anything, sir."

"Who said he did anything? What's your cousin's name?"

"Billy."

"Good. We'll check that. Are you sure he doesn't have another first name?"

"Uh, yes . . . Sefa."

"Good. And what did you do in your group?"

"We reviewed our course work."

"All the time?"

"Yes."

"You expect me to believe that you spent all your time working? You must have had some fun once in a while?"

"A few times, yes."

"Interesting. And the rest of the time, you were focused and studious? Do you take me for an idiot?"

"No, sir."

"So tell me what you did in your free time."

"Nothing much, sir. Walks."

"Where? What neighbourhoods? And what did you talk about in the street?"

"About our exams, about the future, sir."

"You talked about the future? Why?"

"We wondered what it would be like."

"Interesting. So you were afraid."

"A little."

"Why? When you're young, you're not afraid of the future. Had you forgotten that the youth of the Revolution and the Nouvelle Marche must have faith in the future?"

"No, sir."

"So why were you worried?"

"We didn't know if we would pass our exams."

"But if, as you said, you were working all the time, you had no reason to be concerned, did you?"

"Some professors are hard to convince. They don't cut us any slack."

"Slack?"

"I mean they're very demanding."

"And that's a bad thing, in your opinion?"

"No, sir."

"Okay, let's move on. Besides your walks and discussions, what did you do?"

"Nothing else."

"That's not what I learned."

"Uh... We tried a few months ago to do some theatre."

"Now that's much more interesting."

"It was just to have some fun, sir."

"Theatre is serious. What plays did you do?"

"Classics."

"Such as?"

"We never managed to put on a whole play."

"Why?"

"We didn't have time."

"Ah! You would have had to cut down on your walks?"

"Yes."

"What was the last play you were involved in?"

"Césaire. *A Tempest*."

"Why that one?"

"It was about slavery and colonialism."

"You know very well, don't you, that the Revolution has overcome imperialism? And that it's pointless to celebrate the past, that this should be a time of optimism and nation building?"

"That's correct, sir."

"A tempest is a maelstrom. The exact opposite of the peace we have achieved."

"That's true."

"What are the names of your friends? I mean the other three members of your group."

"Uh . . ."

"You're hesitating. Do you know what's happening right now in the capital?"

"No, sir."

"No? They're burning houses. You wouldn't want that to happen to you, would you? You'd like to find your parents and your brothers and sisters safe and sound, wouldn't you? You know, when there's a fire in a house at night, the people often don't have time to get out before it falls down. So, what are the names of your friends? If you haven't done anything, I don't see why you're hesitating. So?"

"Beno, Sika, Wali."

The man suddenly leaned across the table, and his slap jerked my neck around. "You wretch, you're giving me first names. I want full names!" I wiped the blood from the corner of my mouth with the back of my hand and I gave the names of my friends. The man concluded with a smile, "I hope they were good actors, at least."

27

A slight noise at the door. Ito Baraka stops writing. He hopes it's Kimi Blue coming home earlier than usual. He remembers their first meeting. A spring day. On a nasty, rainy afternoon, he had gone to buy a few necessities second hand at Emmaus in Old Hull, where she worked. Out in front of the store, she was putting used clothing into two big garbage cans. He said to her, "I hope you're not going to stuff yourself into those garbage cans with the rags. I think you could still be useful for something." She smiled and asked him if he could help her carry the garbage cans to the back of the store. Ito remembers answering that he once lived in a garbage can, and that when he finally managed to get out, his limbs, naturally, were completely stiff.

Kimi comes from the Indian reserve of Kitigan Zibi Anishinabeg, near Maniwaki, north of Ottawa. After the death of her father, who one day hanged himself from the only tree in the backyard of their house, she ended up for years on her own, taking care of her mother, who was not right in the head, whose lungs were bad, and who was stuck in a wheelchair as a result of a car accident and a dissipated life. Kimi worked at the checkout of a grocery store there, and at the end of the day, she would make a detour to the cabin of a man who supplied mother and daughter with cigarettes, alcohol, and cocaine. Kimi Blue's life consisted of the mother, who was as good-natured as a starving dog, the grocery store, which had been deserted by customers, and powder. Her time had become frozen that way. Time on the reserve was a sky of fixed patterns and an unchanging wind in the impassive maples. Tedium, sometimes with the sense of standing at the edge of the world. That was Kimi Blue's country, her homeland. She lived, she said, in that confinement, and in the reality of a broken thread in her story. She said, "We no longer have any connection to what we were deeply, or what we wanted to be. A new way of being in the world began for us, existing through drinking binges, smuggling, crime, and cannabis. People on the reserve are often arrested for trafficking, narcotics use, or violence. Time, our time, is more and more frozen. One day in May 2007, I left. I abandoned my mother and fled. When I went back a month later, she was dead, and since then, her shadow has pursued me."

She has often told Ito that the farce known as a smile has disappeared from the faces of her people. Their faces have become masks of powerlessness and resignation, and they are motionless actors with roles as extras on their reserve, that remote Native camp that is like a movie set. There are those who drink and those who kill themselves, a brutal death or a slow agony slumped outside their houses throughout the dark days.

Ito Baraka remembers their first evening together, and how shy she was, though she was a good thirty-five years old. He invited her to sit down on the groaning springs of his couch, and for a long time, they said nothing to each other, Ito absorbed in the colourful toes of his slippers and Kimi staring at a point in front of her. Finally, she coughed discreetly and abruptly started talking about herself. The reserve, her family, drugs, her friends, who with nothing to do were fixtures on the corner of King Edward and Murray in the centre of Ottawa, constantly stoned, seeking bread, shelter, and company at a Christian mission with the reassuring name of the Shepherds of Good Hope, masters of those sidewalks where they bought and shared grass and powder behind Christ's back. After her workday at the thrift shop, Kimi Blue would spend time with these friends at that crossroads of the miserable before returning to her modest apartment on a street whose name made you think of salvation, Mont-Bleu. In the evening, she continued with a first smile, she would walk home, her feet light on the stairs of her building because she had just had a hit. She would throw herself still dressed on her bed and take refuge in childhood, when her father had not yet been trapped by whisky, and her mother, who still worked on the Hébert family farm, ten kilometres from Maniwaki, would whistle while she hung out the laundry on a yellow line in the yard, which was filled with hungry birds that she liked to feed. That time before what she called the gradual contamination, by the bottle and the hundred-gram packets that had little by little invaded the homes. She couldn't say who had started selling that shit on the reserve, or why so few people were able to resist it. Ito moved closer to his new girlfriend on the couch, and for the first time she turned her face towards him, looked him straight in the eye, and asked him to open up in turn, to tell her about himself.

Later, Ito got up to offer her something to drink. She asked for coffee, and while he was busy in the kitchen, she went to the bathroom. A good quarter of an hour, he noted, and when she came out, her forehead was damp. She had taken off her big sweater and all she had on her upper body was a tiny, light T-shirt that showed her nipples. And for the first time in a long time, Ito Baraka felt the swelling of an erection between his legs. There were red spots and scratches on the girl's arms, and the hair was clammy with sweat. She felt his desire and looked away. "The coffee's ready," Ito said to break the awkward silence. She sat down again and, after taking a sip from her cup, she began to ask him questions.

Half an hour later, Ito went back to the kitchen to make them omelettes. He returned with the plates, which he set down on the coffee table. He suggested turning on the TV, but she said no. They ate in silence. After the meal, she said, "I know you want to make love. We can try now that we've replenished our strength. The omelette was good." Ito didn't reply, and when he went to return the plates to the kitchen, she got undressed and lay down on the couch. He was going to turn off the light, but she raised herself on one elbow, in a panic, "No, leave the light on!" He got undressed and joined her on the couch, Kimi with her hollow belly and bushy pubic hair. She opened her arms, offering him the gift of her lovely breasts. He lay down awkwardly on top of her, his trunk between her nervous thighs, and with both hands, she pressed his cock mechanically against her vulva to take him inside her. Ito remained leaning on one elbow, slowed down by the brusqueness of the girl's actions. Her dilated pupils seemed to be begging him to go ahead, but he had known some women in his time and he was thinking that this was when most of them closed their eyes to fully experience the intensity of penetration.

The clock in the apartment showed it was past midnight. She asked him to take her to the bed. He did so, carrying her light, frail body. His desire came back. She said, "I'm going to turn over on my belly. You lie on my back. That way you won't be afraid of my open eyes." He refused. In the bed, it was she who got on top of him. She kissed him greedily. She found his cock and tried with difficulty to take into the dryness of her pussy. Disappointed, she collapsed on her lover's chest. Kimi, frigid and hooked on cocaine. He told her she should seriously consider another detox treatment since the first one hadn't succeeded. She promised to think about it, and added that some of her friends at the crossroads of the miserable had, like her, tried to stop. They had failed and had gone back to living on the street. She still had a little grass in her bag, and she got out of bed to roll some joints in translucent paper. She came back under the sheets. It was the first time Ito Baraka had tried grass. He couldn't turn off the light because she was afraid of the dark, and she kept her eyes open so as not to see the menacing shadow of her dead mother.

28

Ito Baraka goes to his work table. He would rather Kimi find him there when she comes home, in the position of someone who is still able to do something with his time. From there he glimpses the back of the apartment door with three coats hanging on it. He crosses the space between the desk and the coats with difficulty, feels the lining of the one in the middle for a hidden pocket, from which he takes a small transparent plastic bag to roll a few joints while he waits for Kimi. It's their little ritual, once a week, and she loves that time, when they sit close together on the sofa and smoke until the middle of the night. They don't talk, each one trying to forget something in the wreaths of smoke, she, a mother devoured by disease and the ashen body of a father at the end of a rope, and he, the creaking of his old carcass. He goes back to the table, gets some rolling papers out of a box, takes the marijuana from the bag, and gets to work rolling the joints. He remembers to wet the edge of the translucent paper. He looks at the answering machine, which is blinking. Perhaps a message from Kimi. He doesn't want to listen to it, he's afraid she'll say she won't be coming tonight. He prefers to wait. He starts to feel a tingling under his skin again and a heavy, slack mass in his muscles. Kimi will find him sitting there, it's impossible for him to move. He leans back in the chair, closes his eyes for an instant, picks up his pen again. The shadow of his friend Koli refuses to let go of him.

———◆———

In the evening, in our cell, I would turn over the slop pail and stand up on it. And beyond the bars I was hanging onto, I could see a slice of the sky at the end of which were the moon, there as always, and a few stars scattered on the canvas of the night, like us in the camps and prisons of the country. The night went by that way. I slept little, and the morning always surprised me with its mocking blue hue. Season after season of captivity, punctuated by the death of a prisoner forgotten by his family, who did not come and get the cadaver, his remains left for three days behind the huts before the guards decided to bury him farther in the bush, or the jubilation of a fellow prisoner who had been waiting a week for the visit of a son or a wife, the guards always drunk and chanting obscenities at the top of their lungs. The unchanging emptiness of Koli's eyes at dawn.

We drifted in a slow agony, our asses glued to the dirt floor of the cell. Inside the barbed wire fence, the sorcerers were dying, scarecrows emptied of their straw by the cruel beaks of the birds of prey under the gloomy gaze of the tall trees above the thickets and yellowed fields. Over our heads, the migration of the birds that I managed not to envy anymore. And sometimes we were visited by a woman, a hooker with lips painted red as in a crime scene. She would go from guard to guard, a Venus with an ass of steel, how else could she handle the fury of the half-dozen enraged guards at the gates of her flesh at the same time? From their cells, the prisoners could hear her yelling at the guards to behave themselves, and we imagined them having to calm down and form a perfectly straight line at her crotch, each one in turn if you please, gentlemen. And in the morning, she would leave, standing very straight, unshakeable. And walking with her to the gate at the entrance of the camp, the head guard would kiss her hand smiling and bowing, "Dear madam, thank you for calming for a time the anger of these cocks exiled far from civilization and any salutary brothels."

The woman was pretty, with smooth, deep black skin, braided hair, and large eyes in a slightly oblong face with thick, smiling, ravenous lips. She was radiant, unlike the other bodies and skins. The bodies of the sorcerers were all dry wood, skin and bone, limbs disproportionately long in a strange process of growth, chests and heads bowed, and when I described them to my blind companion, he observed, "You mean they remind you of Giacometti's sculptures?" I answered, "Yes, Koli, here they make Giacometti bodies, thin, pale, with skin like a shadow on the metal of the limbs." "It's beautiful work," said Koli. "You mean the sorcerers?" "Giacometti. Not the sorcerers, I can't see them."

And from the sorcerers, we went on to the other silhouettes of the camp, which I described to my friend. The head guard, pudgy and short-legged, and his henchmen, with hardly more meat on their bones than the sorcerers, their lips reddened by alcohol, their faces puffy. There was one who limped, a disjointed puppet. And the head interrogator, the man with the pliers, whom we rarely saw outdoors, tall and classically handsome. And the other prisoners, their unimposing bodies worn down by the years. All this to say that in the end, though gaunt, the most beautiful body was that of Koli Lem, whose hair had whitened uniformly and who was still very straight for all his seventy years, his chin square and strong, his nose regular and his forehead broad and free of wrinkles. On evenings when I didn't have much to do, I would spend my time appreciating the beauty of that body, and little by little, every line and feature of my friend became imprinted in my memory, and in the plays that I would later write, all the bodies would look like Koli's, the picture of dignity and noble bearing.

Between the bars of the cell blew a cold, biting wind. Morning came slowly, followed by another night when I would again feast my eyes on Koli with his princely visage. Because everything around us was ugly, the living dead, the yards, the sewer breath of the guards, their spit on the walls and the prisoners, the flights of bats just before nightfall, the brutal relationship with the tortured bodies, all of it ugly, unchanging, tedious. To give my eyes something else to look at, I had only Koli and his face sculpted in iroko wood and displaying a proud serenity that the moonlight could illuminate or dim. That face could reflect life or death, and so that it would not pale on the threshold of death, I had to rub it with my palms and warm it. When we had no more books to read, Koli had to come back to life and tell a story for us as only he could.

29

Ito Baraka clenches his teeth. He's experiencing stabs of pain again, pain that rises until it reaches a climax and he sees the faces of the friends whose names he revealed during his interrogation. He can't stop feeling that what happened to them afterwards is his fault. The pain is infused with shame and remorse. So he drinks.

He remembers that when he had a stomachache as a child, his father would take a long-necked bottle from the cupboard. At the bottom of the liquid in the bottle, there were roots and bark with complicated names. His father would get out a little glass for this sodabi, which could rip out your insides, pour an eighth of a glass, the proper dose, and give it to him. Ito would grumble, but an hour later, the stomachache was gone in a plaintive purr, and he would think, relieved, that this remedy with its obscure roots could cure all ills—indigestion, migraine, angina, diarrhea. But when the real ills of anxiety and distress loomed on the horizon, he had to face the fact that the long-necked bottle could do nothing for them, and his father, powerless, would have to put it back in the cupboard.

Ito knew that the little glass of sodabi could only banish the ills for a while. And later, when the country became unlivable, he drank to keep the frustrations and the leaden sky at bay. You had to stay completely soused, and as soon as you felt the depression and pain coming back, here you go! another little glass of the morphine prescribed

by the gods of wisdom, and here you go again! until your gaze was
clouded, preventing you from taking the measure of your misfortune
in the violence of the streets, like a scene in a movie, a murder or a
rape you'd rather not subject yourself to and on which you lower the
screen of your eyelashes and eyelids, capitulating in the face of the
unbearable. When Ito Baraka started to drink, he would often in his
fog see the magician's fingers of his father pouring the glass of spirits
that freed you in no time at all from what was unendurable, the ill
expelled with a glug-glug-glug and a burp.

In the evening, Ito Baraka goes down into his basement and drops
onto the left side of his sofa, where his bum has hollowed out a nice
depression. His bottle of rum is uncorked. Yes, it's rum or Scotch. To
your health! Straight from the bottle. His blood gives that giggle he
recognizes. The basement where he's gone to ground is more and more
damp, so he has to warm himself up. He absent-mindedly grabs his
antique remote control and turns on his tiny television, which gives a
moan and turns off again. He stretches his legs and Kimi Blue comes
and sits on his lap, her dark head in the hollow of his neck. Kimi,
affectionate and driven by a desperate passion and desire, wants to tell
him about her day. A mirage. He rubs his eyes and she disappears. The
tattered carpet is a devastated battlefield, the yellow paint on the walls
is flaking. Above the TV, two photographs, a smaller one of Kimi and
the little boy, and another, fifty by eighty centimetres, of Giacometti's
sculpture *The Walking Man*, with his long, thin, stiff limbs. He bought
it in a junk shop. Because the work reminds him of Koli Lem, with
whom he first discussed the Swiss sculptor. In recent days, when he
stares at the photograph, he has the impression that the Man is disin-
tegrating more and more, that he's breaking into tiny pieces that are
being swallowed up by the passing of time. But he knows very well it's
just a horrible feeling that arises out of the anxiety hidden beneath his
skin.

So he sinks deeper into his sofa and starts drinking again. He lifts
his head towards the ceiling, which has been invaded by mould in
little blackish stains. In a corner to the left of the TV, his old fridge is

gasping. Already, half the rum has been guzzled up. He sets the bottle down in front of the sofa, stands up, leaning on a soft arm, and tries to make out the door to the bathroom. His muddled head refuses to give things form and substance. He catches his feet in his scarf, which has fallen on the floor, stumbles, tries to steady himself by grabbing the stem of the floor lamp behind the sofa, and spins around it in a ridiculous waltz.

He staggers forward and touches the frame of the bathroom door, his vision cloudy. The toilet bowl lid is a distant white spot that becomes clearer when he rubs his eyes. He'll have to kneel before that blurry object, a confessional in which he will let go of his sins and betrayals and all the shit inside him. With the chalk-white oval of the bowl in front of him, his left knee bends. His right arm outstretched, he's going to manage to lift the lid and lower his head to the yellowish water. His right knee bends in turn and he's leaning over the bowl. The liquid he expels stings his nose and spatters him. His belly is in revolt, his chest on fire, and his hands grip the edges of the bowl. Long minutes go by with Ito Baraka in the thick mists of vomit. He feels like plunging his head into it. A stream of drool in the corner of his mouth, he rears up and his head butts the raised lid. Nothing comes out of his skull, although he thinks it must have split open. He tries to relax and his joints crack. He observes the viscous liquid frothing against the ceramic and he wants to immerse himself in a tranquil pond of fish and frogs. He relaxes, wants to sink and take root at the bottom of that pond. The telephone rings. He tells himself he won't have time to take Kimi's last call, but the ringing continues and he slams the lid closed and tries to stand up. He reels, barely catches himself, and totters to the shelf beside the television where the telephone sits. The ringing phone is a stubborn bitch. Ito Baraka goes to grab the receiver—too late, Kimi is leaving a message, "Hello, big guy! How's it going? Love you. See you tonight."

Listening to Kimi Blue's message, he is surprised to find himself, ridiculously, wanting to cling to life. But, he wonders, until what final night will I be able to keep on going? On the wall of his basement, his son is looking at him, eyes whose limpid innocence terrifies him. He's cold, an electric current chills his spine. He falls back onto the sofa and tries to warm himself with the rum. It goes down the wrong way and he yelps like a beaten dog because the alcohol burns his larynx. He tells himself that Kimi mustn't see him in this state, drenched, soiled.

Like the beggar at the corner of his street, Ito Baraka drinks to reinvent brighter days. That's what he did when Santou, after their last argument, slammed the door, taking the child with her. He applied the same method, nights of drinking that were both sad and exultant. He already felt too weak to keep her from doing it. However, the high lasted only a week, because he was taken by surprise by the absurd hope that Santou would come back with the child. He returned to his deferred play project to convince himself that nothing had stopped, but a few days later, here we go again, another relapse in the lake of brown rum. He shut himself up for a whole week and tried, through an abrupt and cynical return to that Catholic faith instilled by the Franciscan fathers in catechism classes, to pull himself together. He thought of his father with his eyes fixed on the black ink drawings on tracing paper from which his luminous plans for villas emerged.

30

A noise at the door again. Ito Baraka straightens up in his seat. The footsteps go up to the apartment above his. It isn't Kimi Blue. Soon it will be twilight. Ito Baraka sighs. He sometimes imagines himself and Kimi in romantic and very foolish scenes as young lovers. It's evening and the young woman has just come home from work, and the drugs are only a bad memory now. On the other side of the door, she's struggling—click, clack—with the stubborn lock. Ito is sitting on the sofa, he doesn't want to get up to open the door for her. It amuses him to think of her getting worked up on the other side of the door. But finally, the lock yields, and Kimi enters, furious. She jumps on him and puts up a pretence of pummeling him with her ineffectual fists. Ito grabs her by the waist to escape the pretend knock-out blows, and she screams, "Let go of me!" and bursts out laughing. He squeezes her waist. Caresses and ridiculous adolescent tickling, and she laughs louder and orders him, "Stop! Read me what you wrote today!" He refuses, "No, forget about theatre." She feigns disappointment, collapses into his arms, and suddenly, she wants him. They fall down onto the dirty carpet, where they make love. That's a cliché right out of the movies, because love is something Ito Baraka can't do anymore. When he tries, he immediately gets out of breath and his limbs tremble and knock together, like an old man with veiny fingers sitting on his the toilet in his retirement home treating himself to a suicidal masturbation.

It's a pipe dream, a farce, this relationship Ito Baraka imagines himself in with Kimi. Except for the early days, his life with his ex, Santou, was a long series of arguments. Their quarrels were a daily occurrence. One evening, she screamed, "I married a bird. Each time he comes back from one of his pub crawls, he's lost a few more feathers! You come back from your drunken nights high as a kite and bury yourself in our basement, and you're drowning here! You're a bat, Ito Baraka! I've found work as a salesclerk, and a daycare for the kid. I'll give you a little more time, a few weeks, to come to your senses!"

He again made all the promises he could think of, but a week later, he was fired from his teaching because he was screwing up, not performing well, giving his students half-hearted answers, bored with those dunces whose progress was as slow as the first steam locomotive. And the following winter, when Santou made the decision to leave him, he didn't oppose it, because he told himself that it was better not to drag his companion and his son down with him. He considered asking for shared custody, but very quickly let that drop, because the judge wouldn't be able to see how he could take care of the kid. Santou and little Ouyi moved to Toronto, far from the basement that reminded her of the failure and rot of their relationship. Ito Baraka found himself alone holding two sets of keys, and when he met Kimi Blue, he didn't need to get copies made.

He saw his son two months ago. His last trip to Toronto. After having tea with Santou in a sadly silent apartment, he spent the afternoon with the teenager in a park behind some high buildings of dirty, cracking cement. Later, a fine rain took them by surprise, and they returned to the apartment. Before Ito left, a smiling Santou mentioned that their son was always first in his math class. She had won, Ouyi would not be like his father, an obscure, tortured playwright who swore only by Beckett and Pirandello. On the bus home, Ito Baraka fell into an uneasy sleep with the flask in the inside pocket of his coat. He was awakened later by a knee knocking against his. It belonged to a young traveller beside him, a noisy, fidgety boy with headphones that let through horrible, loud music.

Back in his hole, Ito drank more than usual to celebrate his son's rescue by the gods of mathematics. He emptied a bottle and a half of his supply of Barbancourt rum that his friend Manuel had sent him from Port-au-Prince. And true to form, his belly reacted. Half doubled over, he managed to reach the bathroom, undid his belt, pulled down his red and white striped underpants and sat down on the toilet, his head between his knees. His hindquarters whistled, setting the tone for the party. He pressed his belly with his folded arms and the noise stopped and gave way to intense pain in his gut. He closed his eyes and tried to make them face that nothingness where everything ends. His trunk, neck, and head leaning forward, he began to sway to the left and then to the right, a choreography that always soothed him. He opened his eyes onto the floor and straightened up slowly, his back against the lid of the throne. The air was foul.

After getting cleaned up, Ito Baraka pulled his clothes up over his bare thighs, and with the most beautiful stoicism, got back up on his feet and, just as miraculously, made it to his work table. A hiccup came to torment him after the diarrhea, and he thought of Léon-Gontran Damas, the poet of French Guiana, whose childhood and past reappeared "in a hiccup shaking my instinct like a cop shaking a hoodlum." He treated himself to another slug of rum and tried to write a scene.

31

Ito Baraka's fingers are again numb with cold. The joints have been nicely rolled. Kimi shouldn't be long. Ito straightens up and closes the notebook. If she were there, he would dictate the next part of his story to her. The bottle of rum is empty. He tries to measure the strength remaining in his stiff muscles and wonders, to what lofty thought he should devote that timid bit of energy. He picks up the notebook, and before his eyes, he sees the film of the last days he spent with Koli Lem.

———— ◆ ————

Koli had decided it was time to organize my escape. My getaway. As if, in our situation, it would be child's play to make a hole in the wall with my hand and just take off. On the other side of the fence, animal traps and ferocious beasts collected anyone in the camp who chanced that adventure, as the guards would remind us. I remember how, one evening, they'd brought back a runaway. They dragged him in by one leg, because the other one was a lump of bloody flesh, severed in mid-thigh by the long metal teeth of an animal trap. They hauled him back and left him to croak behind the huts, a good three days, at the end of which Providence, in the person of the head guard, came to his aid with a bullet in the head. Escape from the camp, repeated Koli, who must have had a plan.

For a little while, there had been a rumour in the camp that the head guard, the pudgy guy with the walk of a punch-drunk boxer, would soon be retiring. He would, of course, have to be replaced. And in such cases, the head guard, before leaving, would suggest to his superiors the name of a possible successor, preferably to be chosen among his drunken corporals. It would be the second time since Koli Lem had been there that the position changed hands, and all the head guard's underlings coveted the job.

One night, Koli Lem spoke of the sorcerers and the powers they were believed to possess, which some people there called *gbas* or *ebo*, gris-gris, sacred spells or amulets that could make you more powerful than ordinary humans, strengthen your aura, and allow you to bend others to your desires, control their thoughts and movements, and make them go in the direction you want them to. And Koli, who had a certain closeness with the alleged sorcerers shut up in their yard, was ready to gamble that they really did have power, although I was doubtful, because if those wretched old people had so much power, why didn't they get themselves out of this death camp? Koli had approached one of the guards who was a potential candidate to succeed the pudgy head of the camp and directly proposed that the guard organize my escape in exchange for a *gbas* that would enable him to rise in the ranks. A dirty, underhanded scheme. My friend assured him that he had discussed it with the sorcerer, who would provide the *gbas* in exchange for a list of favours, beginning with better treatment. The guard rubbed his hands. "An interesting proposition," he replied. "But maybe you're putting me on! Could you be trying to bribe a loyal servant of the state?" Koli replied firmly, "Who's talking about bribing you, Corporal? I'm simply suggesting you increase your chances of becoming the next head of the camp. You'd have to be very naive to think your colleagues are standing idly by without trying to give fate a little boost!" The guard asked, "Why me, blind man?" Koli: "Let's just say it's because you're not the most stupid one. This isn't the kind of bargain you propose to just any fool." The guard: "I see, I see . . . What's in it for you, old man?" Koli: "I'm trying to help a friend. You and I can be sure of one thing, those sorcerers are sly devils. Do you know what I've heard? That at night, they leave their earthly bodies, take flight over our heads, and go off to a depraved banquet with the owls, where blood flows freely in chalices of sparkling white gold! You know very well, the people of the north call them flying men. So think, if they're capable of doing that, why couldn't they give you a *gbas* or some little spell that would convince the head guard to make a decision in your favour? Don't tell me you don't believe just a little in the power of those sorcerers? Judging by how violently you beat them . . . "

Then I wanted to know a little more about the flying men. "Explain to me," I asked Koli. "Explain what?" he replied. "The sorcerers, their flying, or the night?" I didn't sleep a wink after Koli presented his scheme to me. Obviously, he was taking a risk. The story of magic and secret spells sounded like a hoax, the corporal surely couldn't be fooled so easily, and if Koli, who had finally obtained a few favours in the camp, was found out, he could be sent back to square one, to isolation, pliers, and the "black diet," consisting of no food or drink, and no light. I was worried that he would pay a heavy price for my cowardly escape.

However, my mentor was sure of what he was doing and had begun preparations for the escape. In the prisoners' kitchen, he had scavenged a canvas bag, a gourd of water, some dried coconut, and some cassava flour, which he had secretly brought back to the cell. The provisions were supposed to last me until I got to the first village. He put all his energy into organizing what he called my "release." He whispered, "Yes, we're going to create a new freedom for you!" The days and nights went by, and according to Koli and the corporal's plan, I was to leave in a week, on a national holiday. The guards would drink more than usual, and in the evening they would be snoring like malfunctioning electrical generators. That would be the time to clear out.

Yes, Koli Lem took risks to get me out of hell. That, in my view, explains what subsequently happened to him. I've often thought back to it, survivor's shame sticking to my boots like dog shit. I think back to it and I tell myself that since I, the survivor, have been unworthy of Koli Lem's hopes, since I'm ending up a piece of shit, it would be better to cut my losses. No, my life will not have been worthy of my old companion's sacrifice. And so, every day, I stop on the Alexandra Bridge. Under my feet, the silvery sheet of the Ottawa River. Frozen. I wonder about the thickness of the ice on the water. Would it break if you jumped on it? Would it break enough to let a body plunge straight down into that cold water that should bring a quick death, drowning and hypothermia combined? I ask myself that question. I tell myself the bridge may not be high enough for a person to die right off from the fall on the ice if it doesn't break. I'm transfixed by the white immensity under my feet, its surface free of cracks. The pathway of ice, bare, deserted, white, like a life in which nothing has happened. Nothing beautiful or ugly. I clutch the metal railing of the bridge with both hands, the wind whips my wobbly silhouette, I try to empty my mind.

32

As the night of the planned escape approached, Koli began giving me his final advice. He strongly warned me against going home to the capital, where I would be in danger. Instead, he wanted me to head north towards Burkina Faso. He wrote down the name of a friend who was a nurse in Bobo-Dioulasso. Koli didn't have his address anymore, but he thought I would just have to go around to all the dispensaries and hospitals in the city. I was to find that man, who would put me up and give me a refuge while I waited for better days.

"And," my friend added, "in that new city and that other life, you'll try to live again, but I know that the nights will be difficult for you, disturbed by the haunting memory of what you've experienced here, you'll at times relive the blows and the rape you suffered, the insanity and death you've witnessed in this place, and you'll often ask yourself if you really got away from it. And in the morning, although it will be hard, you'll put it all aside, including us, and try to move on to other things. In any case, it's what most human beings with memory do, they try to wall off things they wish they hadn't experienced and plunge back into the streets of the present. The difference is that, depending on what you've experienced, it can turn out to be more complicated. The images that will persist most in your thoughts will be those of violent death. You'll have to get used to it, Ito, or you'll have to do something with it, or else you'll die. The people who don't go crazy are the ones who make music or books, whatever. The important thing is that you get away from this shit. For the rest of us, you'll be on the list of the disappeared."

The disappeared, the ones of whom nothing remains but absence. And during that time, their families hope. "Who knows?" they say, assembled in front of their houses, "who knows, our dear child might come around the corner of the street with a smile on his lips, his face thinner." "Who knows?" the orphans console themselves, but no one is fooled, least of all themselves, they aren't anywhere close to seeing the disappeared again. The disappeared have been dumped on the high seas and there's no wave crazy enough to bring them back to land. And if by some miracle, they've lost the blocks tied to their feet and they manage to float, if their swollen bodies touch the shore, they'll be stabbed again and sent back to the sharks.

"You'll settle in that city where no one knows you and you'll figure out the best way to shroud your violent dead, and my hope is that you'll draw from the rattling of their bones the music or books that will enable you to keep your head above water." Koli Lem repeated the idea again that night, which was to be the last one we spent together. He wasn't sad, quite the opposite, he was happy and a touch excited. Another morning came, and he went to work in the kitchen, while I joined the other prisoners in the yard outside. I passed the time watching the sorcerers, who were wasting away more and more. I would never forget their bodies of metal and wood.

It was a national holiday, and the millet beer was flowing freely. The guards' eyes were red and they were using strong language, and there was crazy laughter and quarrelling. At one point, the voices rose a notch and I recognized that of the corporal who was the accomplice in my escape plan, in an argument that was reaching an alarming intensity. The pudgy head guard tried to act as referee, the uproar continued, a curse, a punch, a scream, and the corporal was lying on the ground in a pool of his own blood with a knife in his heart. That night, Koli Lem sighed and promised we would try again. We stayed awake, and the next day, Koli was told he had a visitor. It was his nephew, who had reappeared with new books, a dozen of them. But that day we learned we would not be together anymore. I was moved to another cell, which I was to share with a silent guy, and Koli kept the same cell, but with a prisoner the others called Nivaquine, the worst kind of scum, a son of a . . . a real shit!

33

So Koli Lem and I were separated. What happened next . . . Nivaquine. Nivaquine, that bastard. The day after his transfer to Koli's cell, he came up to me in the yard and, sniggering through brutish yellow teeth, told me that Koli had asked him to read to him during the night. I imagined Koli urging him, begging him. But Nivaquine had refused. He never did anything for nothing. He replied something like, "I could read to you, but what will you give me in exchange?" And Koli, without thinking, promised, "Whatever you want." Nivaquine laughed, "Your ass, old man! That's what I want!" Koli gave him the bag that contained the supplies I was supposed to take with me on my escape. Nivaquine gobbled up the flour and the nuts, belched like a half-wit, and told Koli it wasn't enough, he wanted more. Koli called him a devil and demanded that he read him a chapter now that he had eaten everything, but the son of a bitch farted loudly and went to asleep.

During this time, there were rumours circulating in the camp that the situation in the capital was deteriorating, the government had been shaken by a series of demonstrations, and public discontent in the streets was entering a critical phase, which might hasten things in the camp. There was even speculation that they were beginning to close the detention camps, bulldozing them to erase any trace of their existence. Meanwhile, in their cell, Nivaquine began exploring Koli's chest, and as the days went by, Koli finally surrendered a patch of his skin. The scoundrel stroked his upper body and rubbed his belly. Koli remained impassive, undoubtedly focused on the man's promise, "Let me do it and I'll read you a first chapter." Koli, absent from his body, oblivious to the hands running over his torso. And Nivaquine licked Koli's torso and put his tongue in the little holes left by the torturers' pliers in place of his nipples. He bit the blind man, who didn't flinch, and moved from his chest to the hollow of his navel. Koli breathed noisily then and tried again to forget, he went back to his former life, to his last biology class with his students, the sketch of a human torso on the blackboard and the descriptions of the organs, the liver, the pancreas, the heart, the veins, the lungs, all that Nivaquine was trying to bite, with the children repeating the names of the organs. Nivaquine with his slobbering mouth, intoning strange words, in a trance, his hand seeking to go farther than the belly of the blind man, who finally swore and grabbed Nivaquine, who shouted, "You bastard! Okay, no reading for you!"

The next night, Nivaquine's hands went farther than Koli's navel. They advanced toward his lower abdomen and pressed it furiously, and then they descended again and grabbed Koli's cock, erect in spite of himself. And because Nivaquine repeated his promise, the old man let him have his way, it was only a little game of the flesh. Nivaquine bit his glans, and Koli hit him on the neck, but that shit actually enjoyed it and he grunted. With Koli at his throat and one hand firmly gripping Koli's cock, Nivaquine undid his pants and took his own cock in his other hand, twisting and squeezing it. Nivaquine had become the possessor of two cocks. He shook his own and let out a hoarse cry, and the hot, sticky liquid landed on Koli's face. Nivaquine, out of breath, said, "I'm pooped, can't read you anything tonight, we'll see tomorrow." Koli did up his pants, as if anyone could see him or spy on him. He grabbed a book and threw it against the wall, swore through clenched teeth, and kicked into the emptiness, striking the ribs of the bastard, who was already asleep. He dragged himself to the window and grabbed hold of the bars.

The next day, the same rumours were still circulating. The capital was in turmoil and the camps were being closed. As for Nivaquine, his mind was tormented by Koli's body. That night, repeating his promise, he again threw himself on the old man, who was silent and on his guard to make sure the fiend did no more than touch him. Nivaquine went past the barrier of the belt and forced his way between the thighs of his fellow prisoner. Koli had expected the same thing to happen as the night before, but then the ugly ape suddenly got down on his knees, grabbed his feet, and tried to turn him over. The blind old man managed to keep his elbows against the floor before backing away and getting to his feet again. Nivaquine swore and came closer, and Koli could smell the beast's breath. Nivaquine dove for his waist, but Koli managed to dodge his heavy body and Nivaquine banged his head against the wall. He turned around again and pushed Koli into a corner. The old man kneed him in the crotch, and he screamed, grasping Koli's head in his hands and pounding it against the wall over and over.

Koli Lem's shouts aroused the other prisoners, and we heard the guards running in the night. The commotion was followed by a troubling calm, with a burning smell on the wind and whistling and crackling sounds. In the morning, we observed what was left of a fire, in which there were documents still burning. Around ten o'clock, the sorcerers were released, the guards opened the gates of the camp and pushed those old people out into the bush, where they had no chance of survival. I waited in our yard with the other prisoners, and toward evening, the soldiers came and blindfolded us. We were thrown into jeeps, which immediately drove away. We travelled all night long. I never saw Koli Lem again. He must have died.

34

Koli Lem was dead, but everywhere my travels took me, I would see him in other bodies and other eyes. In the cities I passed through, I had a habit of wandering the streets, and after I had honoured my commitment for lectures or workshops, I would roam the urban jungle in search of my friend. Since I hadn't seen his cold body, he couldn't be dead, so I searched for him from Port Said to Durban, and one morning in Bamako, there he was, a newspaper hawker on a sidewalk of the city. He was alone, and his skin was burnished by the Sahel wind. As thin as he was, he was holding his head high. In the street, the plaintive notes of a kora somewhere must have been celebrating our reunion. I introduced myself to the stranger and invited him for tea. It was Koli, for sure. We talked for a good hour on the patio of the café. At first reticent, he told me about his life as a pedlar in that part of Africa. He spoke with the vigour of his forty years, and I wanted to touch him to be sure he was real, to feel his face again and his nearly hairless chest. The next day, I invited him to my hotel room to rediscover the atmosphere of the four walls of the cell we had once shared. He brought me a gift, an amulet that was supposed to protect me from evil spells, and in return I gave him my first published play. He looked at the volume with an indifferent eye and stuffed it into his canvas bag, as if books were unfamiliar objects to him. He had Koli's thick hair and regular features.

He finally took his leave, and from my window, I saw him pulling his newspaper cart in the crowded street. A few months later, I found him again in Gibraltar—no, it was actually in Salvador de Bahia. His body was not as thin, and he was fishing in the waters of the Baía de Todos-os-Santos, dressed in wide white pants, his bare chest gleaming. In the distance, another fisherman had started singing a song. I sat down on the bank and watched the Brazilian, with his heavy muscles, hauling the net up from the depths, slowly, patiently. It was Koli. The man introduced himself, "My name is Zumbi," and continued, "Do you want me to show you Bahia?" I accepted, and the whole next day, we walked on the black cobblestones of the city. He was a fisherman, and a capoeira dancer in his free time. He took me to a backyard where he trained with other, younger guys, because he was already going on fifty, solid and agile in spite of his age. After the dancing, he wanted us to go back to the hotel for a shower. At the hotel, I left him alone under the stream of water, but he asked, "Are you coming?" I backed away, and he got mad and said something like, "I don't understand you!" He came out of the shower furious, threw his towel on the ground, got dressed, and left the room, slamming the door.

Through the course of my travels, I pursued the shadow of blind Koli, and one evening he was in the Paris metro, big sunglasses covering his dead eyes. He was playing the trumpet, and the rare notes that he managed to get out mingled with the rumble of the trains and the noise of the footsteps of the passersby, who threw coins at his feet. The man was playing a mournful solo. I stood to one side to listen to him, and when the spectators from the subway vanished, I went over to him and invited him to Rue des Lombards to a discotheque that offered cautious jazz, Duke Ellington, Thelonious Monk, Charlie Parker.

After the concert, we separated, but I was to see him again in New York, in Havana, in a bar in Amsterdam, where smoke from the fat spliff he was smoking momentarily masked his features, the same ones, and in Mexico City, Toronto, and, a few weeks ago, in the bar in our little city of Hull where I'm a regular now. Very often, I would buy him a drink and we would talk late into the night and I could reassure myself that my friend was not dead.

35

"Did you love Koli?"

"Yes."

"How?"

"The way one loves."

"By touching him, desiring his body?"

"He was blind. Beyond words, it was the only way to make him feel that I was there."

"Did you sleep with him?"

"We slept huddled together when it was cold." "

"You touched him because you loved him?"

"No. Because he was beautiful."

"Is he really dead?"

"I believe so. There was a silence after his screams in the cell."

"But you aren't sure."

"I wasn't able to verify it."

"Because you left the camp."

"Yes."

Ito Baraka remembers, that was how Kimi questioned him about Koli the second time. It was on an evening like any other, after supper, when they were sitting on the broken-down sofa. In front of them, the grey of the bare wall-to-wall carpet reminded Ito of a dance floor where, in other times, he might well have gone dancing with the girl, that rumba that could still take him back to the past, a way to give fate a helping hand and a time for them to settle into the habits of a couple on a Saturday night of music, alcohol, subdued lighting, and the longing to touch. Outside, a timid wind was climbing the sloping street, and the lampposts were flirting with the silhouettes of the bare, exposed trees of January.

36

The lock on the door resists for a minute, then yields. Kimi Blue comes in holding a paper bag. She pushes the door closed with her foot. He can see her slender back and her jet black hair. She turns and smiles and jerks her head to flick away the stray lock of hair over her left eye that's preventing her from seeing the man at the table in the shadows of dusk. She turns on the light and comes over to run her freed hands—she has set the bag on the table—through Ito Baraka's thick head of hair. He responds by putting his arm around her waist, and she pulls away a bit to look at him. She can see that he has lost more weight since their last evening together two days ago. He's breathing noisily and looking at her in silence. She wants to warm up the food, which has cooled, and heads to the tiny kitchen between the bedroom and the bathroom. She says, "I'll be back in ten minutes. You'll tell me about your trip while we eat." Ito Baraka watches her moving around. Kimi has put on her slippers. She appears fragile at one metre sixty, with her tiny waist and her young girl's jeans. The clatter of pots and pans fills the apartment. Ito opens his notebook again. He feels the evening fever coming on. His throat hurts too. The lines he has just written in the dim light are not very straight. He feels like vomiting again, holds back. He wants to continue his story, it's a stubborn player that won't give up the game even though failure is imminent. Again, the illusion of fleeing his painful body through words.

— ◆ —

Hours after we left the camp, our jeep was still travelling through a rural region. I could sense it from the persistent smell of cut grass and wet earth and the characteristic rustle of trees. There were four of us in the vehicle. I heard the driver curse from time to time because of the state of the road—we were no longer moving on asphalt—his swearing supplemented by that of his colleague, who was supposed to keep us under control in the back. I was not the only prisoner in the vehicle, another person's breathing was superimposed on mine, and it quickened when the driver said to his colleague, "We'll be there soon, get ready. Relax, the map doesn't show any villages around here. You're going to be okay. I know it's the first time for you, but it'll go quickly. Just remember that these are orders." The other man replied in an uneasy voice, stammering. "Yes, sergeant. But . . . I see fields, cleared areas between the trees." "Impossible," replied the driver, "it's forest here, and besides, I've already been to this region." "I swear, sergeant, there are cleared areas, we might run into people." "Stay calm, corporal, it won't take long. Orders are orders."

It was clear that they were going to liquidate us in the woods. I began to sweat. Under my bum on the seat I felt a warm liquid, the other prisoner had pissed himself. I didn't have time to gauge the unpleasantness of the situation, because the sergeant braked suddenly and the vehicle stopped. He gave brief instructions to the corporal, "Get out of the jeep and take the shovels, and lock the doors behind you." "Yes, sergeant!" I found myself alone in the vehicle with the other condemned man, and a minute later, we could hear the sound of the shovels against the earth, and their voices. The sergeant said to his subordinate, "Keep working, I'm going to take a look around." The corporal continued with the task, and at one point we heard him say in a frightened schoolboy's voice, "Forgive me, Lord, they're orders, there's nothing I can do about it, forgive me." The sergeant returned from his round. "Here, go on, have a drink, corporal, it'll make it easier. Take a good slug!" They picked up the shovels again, and for a quarter of an hour, we didn't hear their voices. The boy beside me said in a panicked voice, "My name is Kézié, what's yours? They're going to put a bullet in our heads, they're going to eliminate us!" I told him my name, and said nothing more.

The sergeant spoke again, "That should do it, it's deep enough. Phew, this is gruelling! We could have asked those bastards to dig the holes themselves, but they take too long, they drag it out and really try your patience." The doors of the jeep opened again, and the corporal ordered us to get out. He said to his superior, "Sergeant, do you hear that? It sounds like footsteps." "Impossible, there's nobody within ten kilometres." "Yes there is, listen." Footsteps were indeed approaching. The sergeant hissed through his teeth, "Shit! Get in the jeep!" At the same time, Kézié started running, and I followed him unseeing, still blindfolded. The jeep roared to life and I bashed my head against a tree trunk.

I stayed there for several minutes with my face against the rough bark, expecting my neck to be shattered by a bullet from the corporal. Footsteps again, advancing hesitantly through the bushes. Then hands, with exasperating slowness, removing the blindfold from my eyes. I found myself face to face with an old man who must have been around eighty. A few metres behind us, Kézié was sitting in the grass weeping, his knees together, trembling. Two women were standing beside him, and one handed him a gourd of water. At their feet were two huge bundles of firewood. The old man said, "My name is Mambou. Come on, let's go." And for a good five kilometres, we staggered after Mambou and the two silent creatures with the firewood, whom he introduced as his wives. We came to a hamlet and the older of the wives went and got a mat from a hut and Kézié and I collapsed onto it. The old man lay down on his reclining chair and told the other wife to bring him tobacco, while the first one prepared to light the stove. Kézié was trembling less, the morning was drawing to a close. I sat up and watched Mambou smoking his pipe. The old man looked at me and murmured, "You can tell me about it if you want."

Which I did after the meal. The women remained silent, and after

I finished my story, the old man said, "We're in the central region. Tomorrow morning, I'll take you to the highway and you'll be able to get a ride in one of the trucks going to the capital." Kézié had barely touched the food prepared by the women, who, after serving us and eating themselves, had gotten to work weaving baskets. Mambou went into his hut for an afternoon nap. I continued watching the women work, and Kézié went to sleep on the mat. Dusk came quickly, we had another meal, and I went to sleep beside Kézié in the hut of the young wife. She had joined her octogenarian husband, who apparently hadn't yet lost certain habits.

In the morning, Mambou asked us to help him take the baskets the women had made to the highway, where he was going to try to sell them. It must have been six or seven o'clock. We walked for an hour on increasingly narrow trails that finally led to the cracked asphalt of National Highway 1. We squatted in the grass beside the road like guerillas preparing to attack. A few cars and heavier vehicles passed us without stopping. Two hours later, a truck carrying big bags of charcoal stopped about a hundred metres from our observation point. The driver, a bearded potbellied guy, bought Mambou's baskets after laborious negotiations that must have lasted a good ten minutes, after which I had a feeling the old man had been taken in. He asked the truck driver if he could give us a lift, and the man, suspicious, replied, "They look strange, where do they come from? I don't want any problems." Mambou tried to reassure him, "They're my grandsons, they're going back to the capital." "I see. Can they unload bags of charcoal?" "Don't judge by their appearance, they're strong." And without further ado, the old man said goodbye to us and headed back along the trail. The driver told us to climb up on top of the bags and started his truck, which moved off at the pace of a dying donkey.

37

After leaving old Mambou, we drove to the capital. I found myself on an avenue packed with pedestrians and street vendors. It must have been eleven o'clock or noon, and I headed towards the seashore. There was no crowd at the beach. A little albino boy was napping in the shade of a coconut tree and two girls were arguing and laughing their heads off. There was a metallic glint on the surface of the water in the distance. I sat down on the sand, my arms around my bent knees, my toes lapped by the dying waves. But very soon, I no longer saw the open sea before my eyes. I was thinking back to Koli, imagining him sitting beside me and asking me to describe the scene to him.

So I described to my friend the ridiculously blue waves, the fishermen and rowers coming back to shore, the line of sweating men pulling in nets, accompanying their task with songs repeated in chorus, the women sitting on an overturned pirogue, each waiting to be the first to bargain for the fish, the laughter, the loud voices, the two lovers perched at the end of the wharf, and the young man sitting beside it plucking the strings of an ancient guitar. I described that beach scene to Koli, the cheers of the men, who had succeeded in pulling in a net filled with seafood, the rush of the women for the sardines, carp, skate, tuna, tilapia, shrimp, crab, and herring, and the fishermen paying the men who had helped them. What I presented to Koli was a country of my own invention, because the nets were now empty, the fishermen bitter, and at the end of the wharf there were not lovers but a father worn out by his many burdens, getting ready to throw himself into the waves.

From the shore I headed to our neighbourhood on the outskirts. In the Hanoukopé district, I walked along the abandoned railway line. A pair of beggars went limping down the middle of the track, begging bowls in their hands and offspring hanging onto their big tattered boubous. Snot dripped from the kids' nostrils, darkened by the dust-filled air. They were breathing black dust from a little charcoal market along the railway track, which had piles of bags punctured during transportation or by little pilferers. Roaming kids would help themselves to the charcoal and resell it a few sheds farther on to a stout old woman who cooked bean fritters and cornbread in a stove.

When I arrived in front of our house, I stood staring at the door for several minutes before opening it. My father, who wasn't working that day, saw me from the terrace and dropped his reading glasses. He got up from his chair and shouted my name. Behind the house, there were hurried footsteps, and my mother appeared with a shriek and threw herself on my bony, ghostly body. My father stood to one side, a tear in the corner of his eye, while my mother hugged me till I could hardly breathe. My brothers and sisters weren't at home, they'd gone out to get food. My father went to get another chair and sat me down, and my mother started circling the revenant in a strange ritual, feeling my body, my face, my belly, my muscles, while her breathing accelerated. My father stopped her, saying, "How about getting him something to drink?" Looking at me, he said, "Don't say anything, we have all the time in the world."

He was the one who spoke. He told of the dead and the disappeared. For the dead, things were settled, but for the others, those who hadn't been found, no one could know. No way to track them down. My father had spent months harassing the police and carrying out fruitless searches wherever he could. He'd made long journeys into the interior of the country, questioning people, and twice he'd also gone to the neighbouring countries, especially those to the west, where people said there were training camps for young fighters. Perhaps I had decided to join the ranks of some obscure rebellion, he thought, to return to the back alleys of the country with a gun and a masked face.

The next day I went into the city to visit my friends. I was reunited with my little world, Beno, Sika, and Wali. I felt uncomfortable, because I knew I had ratted on them. But they were overjoyed and did not seem to notice my shifty traitor's eyes. I asked for news of Gueule de Bois, our mentor and printer of our leaflets. Sika coughed and said he had been found in a drainage ditch with his throat slit. His computer had been stolen and they had tried to burn down his office. Many houses had been set on fire after the riots. At night, organized groups had lists of the homes they would burn. Old people who couldn't escape the flames were asphyxiated and burned to ashes. There were thousands of handicapped people, paraplegics, amputees, and those with other injuries. The number of cripples had mushroomed.

My friends spoke of camps in the interior of the country. From there, too, people returned diminished—or never returned. And names of detention sites circulated, Otadi, Kazaboua, Agombio. People often came back blind, my friends said, their eyes dead for some obscure reason, and when they got home, they could no longer see what their house looked like or observe with their own eyes if it had remained intact or was damaged. They would feel their way along the walls and through the doors, but they didn't actually know, and they still had in their heads the image of the house they had left and that couldn't have changed. They now lived in nostalgia for that hut from the time before, nostalgia for an unchanged world, which was immutable in their heads and their memories as discredited deportees. They were cut off from the new order of things, and the trick would now be to re-establish the connection with that unsettling order—or disorder. And it must be said that very few of us managed it, even with good eyes in the full light of day, we found ourselves blind, like Koli and Hamm, desperately groping our way along the walls of this new world in the hope of finding markers, signposts, traces by which to relearn how to move forward. We walked into the walls, going around in circles, and in that rotation, the land, the country in our heads, was no longer facing the sun in the morning. And night after night we continued the rotation, lost to ourselves and others.

38

Kimi has finished warming up supper. Ito Baraka pushes the notebook aside and stares without appetite at the contents of the plate she has set on the table. He knows he'll barely touch the chicken and steamed vegetables. He'll spend his time examining the face of the woman across from him in the hope of understanding the mystery of her stubbornness, why she persists in playacting at a normal life with him, with its little habits and rituals, the things they enjoy doing together because it gives them what is known as pleasure and a joy that makes you dream of thousands of other seasons of happiness to come, love and laughter under the sun, rituals like their Friday night dates.

A few days ago, they went out and spent the night in a bar in Old Hull listening to the sad music of a saxophonist. And because they had gone a bit far with the Scotch, they returned home at dawn wrecked, but terribly excited, happy. In the morning street, Ito Baraka sang a bawdy song at the top of his lungs, with Kimi trying to respond to the verses. Ito was clowning around, his voice loud, his arms raised in a big V for victory, because they had come close to Heaven and Grace. At one point Kimi tripped on a branch and they almost ended up sprawled on the slippery pavement. She swore loudly, and they hobbled home. Ito said, "If I had the strength, Kimi, I'd write you a play, with a role just for you, as the dawn, light, and happiness! It would be the story of a florist with a stall on a sidewalk. Early in the morning, the customers crowd in front of your stall filled with roses. You tie happiness up for them with flowers and smiles, you sing in the cold morning, and with a sweep of your arm, you show your first customer the variety of your roses. Then you choose the most beautiful ones and make a bouquet, and so on, your mood growing happier and happier as your imaginary customers come and go." A few moments later, Kimi stopped short in the middle of the street. Suddenly serious, she said, "You know, I've never been to the theatre."

"You should go."

"I've heard that in the theatre the actors play at inventing a different life. I don't believe in that. Life, lived in shit or in light, is imposed on you. That's all there is to it. Take detox, for example. I believe that's a way to reinvent your life. Well, it doesn't really work. You always get hooked again. It may be possible to change the lives of others around us, but not our own. Especially when that life is already rotten. Like mine. You can't get anything out of rot, Ito. There's nothing my friends and family can give me. A long time ago, we were burned up from the inside."

"You're wrong, girl. Back home, it worked for some people. They went on the stage, they acted, and they began living again. They found their true place there. And what if that's the problem, Kimi? Things have gone wrong for you because you aren't in your true place?"

"Our place is the reserve. I stayed there for years and I saw nothing good come out of it. And you're not going to ask everyone to go on stage, are you?"

"Your true place, Kimi, your home. Think a little in terms of a home and not the reserve."

"I can see you really did philosophy. And were you really an actor? On a real stage?"

"I tried."

"What did you play?"

"An old man stuck in a trashcan. A crippled old man. "

"A little like you are now."

"Except that now it's not theatre. Let's say the role I'm playing is staying alive."

"Oh, you're going to get better. And we'll take a trip. Tell me, have you ever tried to go back to your house in Africa?"

"It's not the same house anymore."

"It's been rebuilt?"

"It's in ruins now. Everyone who lived there is gone."

"You said your mother was still alive. She didn't leave."

"No. She stayed."

"And you never went back to see her."

"She wouldn't have recognized me. I've changed."

"Didn't you miss her?"

"Every day."

"So you could have gone back."

"A few weeks after my cancer was diagnosed, I bought a ticket. But I was already too worn out to make the trip. It takes two flights and twelve hours of waiting on a bench at an airport."

"But you could have tried."

"I tried."

"Was there a girl you loved in your country?"

"You're changing the subject. That isn't what we're talking about, Kimi."

"I know. So?"

"She didn't want me."

"Why not?"

"She said it was to protect me. She was a prostitute."

"And where are your brothers and sisters?"

"Scattered all over the world."

"They all left home?"

"Yes."

"You told me you were a prisoner in a camp."

"Yes."

"What was it like?"

"A violent, motionless time."

"And that's where you met Koli."

"Yes."

"Was it hard?"

"On my body."

"Only on your body?"

"I'm cold, Kimi. Can we go home?"

"You go ahead!"

And without waiting for Ito's reaction, she rushed toward the back-yard of their building. He followed her laboriously. When he finally managed to get to the yard, she provided a strange spectacle. She had opened one of the big blue recycling bins and was pacing the area with her head down. Ito wanted to know what she was doing. She turned to him, her eyes shooting daggers. He backed away. "What am I doing?" she replied. "I'm doing what you did, I'm acting. I'm throwing the people in my life into this garbage can. My alcoholic father, my mean, crazy mother, my junkie loser cousins, my friends who live at the Shepherds of Good Hope, my first boyfriend, who showed me how to shoot cocaine, all of them, I'm throwing them in, and believe me, they don't mind. You were talking about finding our true place? Well, this is it! We've done it. You can congratulate us." And she started throwing everything she could pick up into the blue bin, frozen boots, a bicycle wheel, empty beer bottles, boards. Ito told her to calm down, she would wake up the neighbours. She continued filling the garbage can, then stopped suddenly, burst into tears, and ran towards the apartment.

39

After the meal, they sit on the couch again. Ito Baraka listens to the sound of his bones knocking together. "Read me what you've written," says Kimi. He doesn't have the strength. Or he'd rather devote what's left of his strength to dictating his story to her. He's trembling again. The fever. Kimi comes over to him and places a hand on his sweaty forehead. He asks her to get the notebook. She hesitates. And without waiting for her reaction, he starts to dictate the next part of the story to her. Kimi has no difficulty following him, he's speaking slowly. She only wonders if everything he's telling her is part of his life story, and to what extent invented people, places, and things have come to the rescue of his memory, which is following the same path of decline as his body, and how much the friends, the fears, the streets, the blood and its smell that he describes are true or false.

——— ◆ ———

A few days after my return home, I headed inland again, to the village Koli Lem had said was his. After a dozen hours on the road, the minibus I had taken stopped in the little town where Koli had been a schoolmaster. I slept in the only motel in the place, a building with narrow rooms and an unusually low roof. When I got up, I offered the owner, a man in his forties, some money to take me to my friend's village on his motorcycle. Along the way, we encountered some school children. The man left me in front of the first house in the village and promised to come back for me in an hour. I walked from there to the middle of what seemed to be the main avenue of that lost homeland. Not a soul in view. It was morning and the peasants must have been in the fields. I walked straight ahead. On either side of the street, the same adobe huts with thatched roofs, a few of them covered with sheet metal. The wind raised the ochre dust.

Then I noticed a thin, almost scrawny man coming towards me, carrying a hoe over his right shoulder and a machete in his left hand. He was walking very slowly, holding his head straight, and when he came face to face with me, he stopped. He spat to the side and said, "You're not from the village." I answered that I was looking for Koli Lem's hut. The man asked, "You mean schoolmaster Koli?"

"Yes, I'm a friend, I used to know him."

"Where?"

"In a camp."

"Schoolmaster Koli disappeared a few years ago. He hasn't been seen since. I was his student and I remember that at the time we were preparing for our primary school certificate exams. Some soldiers came and got him, and there's been no trace of him since. A week after his arrest, people came at night and set fire to his hut. It's the last one on your left, at the end of the road. We put out the fire to protect our own huts."

He asked me again to tell him where and how I had met Koli. Then he murmured, "He must be dead. No one in the village has heard of that camp. Everyone who knew about it must have kept silent for fear of reprisals. Yes, schoolmaster Koli must be dead." I answered, "I believe so. We got separated." Koli Lem's former student added that the hut had not burned down completely and no one had touched the debris, out of respect for the village teacher and because they hoped he would come back. The man walked with me to the house and then left.

The thatch had been consumed by the fire, but part of the charred frame was still standing in spite of the years and the weather. The wooden door was bleached and crumbling in places. I pushed it and it opened to the inside without resistance. The bed in the right-hand corner of the room had also been partially destroyed, the mattress was yellowed and covered with mildew stains, and there was a drinking glass on the dirt floor. On a bedside table were an oil lamp and a clay pipe. Across from the bed, there was a pair of pants hanging from a clip on a clothesline. The rest of the clothes had slipped off the line and formed a rotting pile on the ground. Behind the clothesline, two trunks sitting one on top of the other, the one on top padlocked. I picked it up and set it down beside the second, which I opened.

I wasn't surprised to find books inside. A dog-eared Flaubert, a Fuentes in several volumes, a Pasolini spread open at the bottom, a Lao-tzu (it was the first time I had seen anything by him), *The Brothers Karamazov*, a Conrad, Lévi-Strauss's *Tristes Tropiques,* and a lot of others. I closed the trunk and managed with a lot of effort to hoist it onto my shoulder, it was that heavy. I thought Koli would have wanted to give the books away. I went back to the main road of the village, and at the end of it, the man with the motorcycle was waiting for me in the shadow of the first hut. After some hesitation, he agreed to load the trunk on the handlebars and gas tank of his machine. As we headed back to the city, I asked him to make a stop at the school where Koli had been a teacher. I intended to give them the books, but when we reached the school, I changed my mind, because it was obvious that they weren't reading material for primary school kids. Back at the motel, I gave the money I had left to my host, who agreed to make a final trip to the village to pick up the other trunk.

I took the minibus back that afternoon. The next day, at home, I broke the padlock on the second trunk. It held notebooks, a dozen of them, containing my friend's observations and reflections, and underneath them, some pages held together with elastic bands, the manuscript of a novel, I immediately realized. Pages filled with handwriting that had to be Koli's. On the first one, in big red letters, the title, which reminded me of the strange expression my friend had used for the sorcerers in the camp: "The Flying Men."

In it, Koli told the story of a little boy from an African savannah who had spent the first ten years of his life tending cattle and following the flights of airplanes in the vast sky on their way to faraway places. At twelve years old, when he was sent to school, the boy wanted to become an aviator like Jean Mermoz and Antoine de Saint-Exupéry. However, he lost his parents very early and had to give up school in order to survive. He went back to tending cattle for a quick-tempered uncle. In the sky, the airplanes continued their flights, and the boy was unhappy. But one day, he met a solitary old man, for whom he started providing a few everyday essential services. One night before the man died, he said to the child, "I know your dream, you want to fly. Come, bring your ear close to my lips." And the old man gave him a spell that he was to recite at night in his bed with his eyes closed. When he recited the words, the child found himself in the sky above the trees, houses, rivers, and towns. He could go wherever he wanted, from Pondicherry to the Cape of Good Hope, but he had strict instructions to always come back to his physical body before dawn, or else he would find himself wandering above the clouds for the rest of his days. He only had the right to travel at night. But one night, the boy had a desire to see what the towns looked like in the light of day. He chose not to return to his physical body and found himself suspended for eternity above the Red Sea, near the Bab el-Mandeb Strait.

A story of disarming simplicity, which I read to my friends, who found the style much too classical. Thinking about the flying men, I remembered something that had seemed to me to be just one of the many tortures the sorcerers in the camp were subjected to. Some nights, the guards would smear their bodies with burning peppers, in order, the pudgy head guard claimed, "to prevent their cunning, rebellious spirits from returning to them, and to deprive their travelling souls of bodies." And the guard continued, "When you don't have a body anymore, there's not much you can do, you can't influence the course of events in life." That's what happened to my friends, who were deprived of body and memory.

40

Last night, half asleep, I saw them again. My friends. As if in a dream. I should mention I had news of them a few years ago through my cousin Sefa. He told me that shortly after I left the country, Wali had been hit by a drunk driver on an avenue. After two weeks in a coma, he had opened his eyes, his eyelashes fluttering feebly under the fluorescent fixtures of his hospital room, the harsh light showing his mother what would now be her son's life. Ironically, Wali, who'd had the role of blind, paralyzed Hamm in *Endgame*, had become a piece of furniture displayed in front of their house in the Bé neighbourhood by a resigned mother, who had hung around his neck a rosary with shiny transparent beads that gave him a papal air. And he would bat anxious eyelashes on the world around him, at passersby and fidgety kids, and it wasn't theatre anymore. Although, seeing him so immobile and attentive, you'd have said he was waiting for his cue from another actor. Wali, soft flesh propped up against a tricycle.

Things weren't great for Beno either. Shortly after Wali's accident, he began to walk the streets of his neighbourhood with a bundle of crumpled newspapers under his arm, his hair unkempt, skimpily dressed in shorts and a tank top, which he later dropped to go naked. Or at best with just some scraps of fabric around his waist like Christ the martyr on Good Friday. There was talk of mental strain, and the family did try to lock him up in the house after successive treatments

by a healer, an old priest who was a friend of his father, and an imma-
ture psychologist, which did nothing to stop his deterioration. The
bundle of newspapers under his arm continued to grow, and he would
plant himself in the middle of a road, smooth out the papers and read
the news and events of the day out loud. And once his task as a news
broadcaster was fulfilled, he would carefully fold his newspapers and
start running toward a virtual finish line in the distance. And there
were those who swore he could be seen all over the city, in Amoutivé,
in front of Collège Saint-Joseph, in Agoué, in Djidjolé, but in particular in Tokoin, around the high school and the roundabout with
the huge white marble dove. He had set up his headquarters near the
dove, and it was said that at regular intervals, he would remove his
loincloth and take a shit at the foot of the huge stone bird. He was agitated and loud, and many times, the police came and picked him up.
He would disappear for a week, but finally reappear, calm and docile.
He would sit against the base of the statue with his arms stretched out
along his extended legs, and he could have been mistaken for his paralyzed friend, Wali.

Things were different for Sika, but just as extraordinary. She married a soldier, in what was considered a good match. She didn't finish
her studies. Sika, a housewife and mother of an army of six feisty kids.
The colonel with the red beret married her in a sumptuous wedding
and set her up in a big house on the outskirts of the city. He must
have told her, "In my house, women don't work. You won't want for
anything, *ma chérie*, my little firebrand." And after the wedding, Sika
began to hatch her chicks and get bored, and later, when the children
were in school, she parked herself in front of a huge TV screen that
took up a whole wall of her garish living room and devoured, via sat-
ellite, those series that would deaden the mind of a genius in no time
at all. Sika stuffing herself with fritters in front of the TV and guz-
zling Pepsi-Cola and beer. She had become huge, like Big Momma in
the movie with Martin Lawrence, lugging around rolls of flesh, with
a big potbelly, elephant legs, and a greasy neck like an accordion. She
would get drunk and try to forget the cute young girl she had been,

sighing like a punctured inner tube and saying, "If my father had been alive, he wouldn't have let me marry that lout with his tropical Légion d'Honneur!" And very often, she would end up falling asleep on the sofa.

That was the latest news of my friends, Wali immobile in his chair, Beno limp against the marble pedestal of an imperturbable stone dove, and Sika like a hot air balloon stranded in the thicket of comfortable tedium. And sometimes, the birds of a pointless remorse came and pecked at the balloon of her flesh, which began to lose its air in little farts through every pore. And her fat ass that in the evening would welcome with full honours the colonel on his return home from work. You could say it was endgame for Ito Baraka and his friends, children of the Green Revolution, the agricultural awakening that produced on an African coast a generation of young people who lolled around day after day in front of family homes they still hadn't left at forty years of age, whistling the refrain of waiting through their decayed teeth while successive economic crises weakened hearts and purses that had long been empty. They waited with a feeling of having been screwed by that wily angel that had promised them change, a new, just world, etc. And the tail of the angel continued to smash their last illusions.

41

Ito Baraka breaks off his story, struck again by the devastating current shooting through his veins. His limbs tense and stiffen. Then the cold sweat returns. His jaw clenches. The current grabs him by the belly, a dismal rumbling. A lump rises, he grits his teeth and staggers to the bathroom. From the sofa, Kimi hears him emptying himself. Then, nothing. She knows he has sat down with his back against the bowl. Ten minutes to regain a little control. She won't go check on him. He doesn't want her to. She examines the Giacometti on the wall with a neutral eye. Ito comes back and lies down, his head close to her thighs. He asks her to pick up the notebook again.

She refuses, and goes to get herself a glass of water. She comes back with two thick blankets and covers Ito Baraka from head to toe. With the cold, he feels his sore throat coming back, hammer blows in his head, and steel teeth gnawing at his joints. He bites the blankets and clenches his fists. Kimi turns her head and wipes away a tear. Ito is relieved that she doesn't display the noisy, resounding suffering of the inconsolable mourners in the funeral parlours of his childhood. She says, "Tomorrow we'll go back to the hospital. This time, the doctor will have to keep you there. No way you're leaving after just a few days of treatment!"

Ito Baraka grumbles in protest. Kimi stands up and takes a few steps across the carpet. She glances out the window. The neighbour across the way is smoking in front of the entrance to his building. She goes back to the desk and picks up the joints. She returns to the window and smokes, alone. Ito seems to be sleeping, his breath whistling. He moves, then suddenly becomes motionless. And Kimi, watching him, understands. That it will soon be the end of the story. The day of reckoning when the dead and the survivors are counted. It's clear that Ito Baraka belongs to the latter category, that sad, illustrious breed of miraculous creatures who bear open wounds, haunted by the nights of torture and the horrible metamorphoses of the bodies they lived with in prison camp, those silhouettes that dry out and pile up over time, logs with a large nut at one end that vaguely reminds you of a head. And each time Kimi Blue finds herself facing the photograph of the Giacometti on the wall of the apartment, she inevitably has the same thought, that it is not of a metal object but of a living creature, a prisoner whose veins have finally given up their last drops of blood.

She approaches the inert shape on the sofa and shakes it. Ito slowly opens his eyes. It will soon be over, and Kimi Blue decides she will stay with her friend to the end of his story. She says to him, "I'm willing to keep going if you promise you'll go back to the hospital tomorrow." But Ito Baraka is no longer listening. He is again lying stiff on the sofa, dead wood.

42

Ito Baraka is a flying man. From the sky above the apartment he's looking down at his body lying on the sofa. That scene is followed by another one. It's a Friday night, and Kimi Blue is sitting at a table in the bar they usually go to. The man sitting across from her is a *poète maudit*, a playwright, and he's coming to the end. From the sky, Ito Baraka observes his own character, holding Kimi Blue's hand. On the stage of the bar, the saxophonist they've come to hear is playing, and the words of the song give Ito a familiar shiver: "The women, the women, are rocking their children / And the men are lighting their pipes / And night is falling over the village . . . " A song of nostalgia, into which the authors, Manu Dibango and Akofa Akoussa, have tried to inject a little joy. Kimi asks her man to dance. Ito Baraka thinks it would be a big mistake. He'll collapse after a few steps. But he answers, "That's an offer I can't refuse, isn't it? Come what may, I'll follow you, my lady. Okay, here we go. You'll have to excuse me for being so heavy in your arms. It's just that I have to kind of hang on to you. Do you want to know if it's true what the song says about the village?"

"Yes. I have the impression it's a time and a world that no longer exist. That makes you sad and you whine like a little kid. So what was it like in the village?"

"I grew up in the city."

"But do you know villages? Have you been there?"

"Yes. We spent the summer vacation in a village. And believe me, it wasn't at all boring. The two months went by in a flash."

"How did you spend your time?"

"Clowning, fooling around, kids' games, splashing in mud puddles. The most beautiful times were in the evening. After supper, we'd sit in the middle of my grandparents' yard around a big wood fire. The flames would turn the thatch of the roofs golden and my grandfather would tell us stories."

"What kind of stories?"

"You know, I've forgotten almost all of them. Adventures about jungle animals. They were exciting, but we were scared. Around the fire, grandfather's voice would be booming."

"What scared you? The old man's voice or the jungle?"

"Both. And later, I understood that the jungle was not what I thought it was. After grandfather died, we often went back to the village. There was always a fire in the middle of the yard. The fire was lonely and sad because there was no one sitting around it."

"Why?"

"The times had become dangerous. There were kidnappings, executions, rapes. The party was cleaning house and you couldn't hang around outside at night and tell any kind of story."

"So why did you keep on making a fire?"

"You have to have a fire at night. To keep away the wild animals. They could come and prowl around the huts. Oh! Excuse me, I'm crushing your toes."

"It's nothing."

"We had to keep away darkness and harm. You should do the same."

"Meaning?"

"Carry a flashlight when you go home alone at night."

"Why?"

"To keep harm away, to dissuade potential attackers from getting close to you. A flashlight and a whistle to rouse the neighbours in case of a problem."

"You see danger everywhere."

"Yes. The streets of the world are no longer what they were. Especially at certain hours."

"Go on, this is fascinating."

"No, I have to go and sit down. I'm feeling wobbly."

43

On the sofa, Ito Baraka starts moving again, and opens his eyes. On his lips, the hint of a strange smile. Kimi notices, and looks at him inquiringly. Ito grimaces, "Take notes, Kimi." The young woman is upset but does as he asks.

— ◆ —

According to the latest news, the madman, the one we used to call the Walker, has reappeared around Hanoukopé Market, with the same habits and rituals he was known for. He has started taking his morning walks in the neighbourhood again, beginning at six o'clock, going back and forth delivering his litany of insults to the nation, which he says is sleepy and spineless, and repeating his eternal call, "Revolution or nothing, my friends!" The words hammering in the morning mist, his voice rising and swelling, and swelling till it explodes in the middle of the market, filling the space, the men, and time with its breath of death. Because, even though they say he's the same man, the old Walker I knew in my adolescence, I have trouble believing he's still alive. He must be dead, and it's a ghost who comes to put on a show in the streets in the mornings. He's dead and rotting with his antiquated dream of revolution, that's why they say it stinks when he goes by, and the fetid odour and the insults he scatters all around stick to your skin and your clothes like remorse or shame that is hard, if not impossible, to be rid of.

That's what I was told the last time I had news from back home. They say the old man yelled so loud that the young people have gone back to occupying the streets and roadways, their fists raised, discontented and determined to overturn the tropical order of things that don't work, and in the sky, the sergeant with the Uzi watches them from his helicopter, and when the spectacle annoys him, he fires into the crowd of schoolkids and older people and on all who refuse to obey, but new threatening fists are raised toward his chopper in the sky.

During this time, in other neighbourhoods of the city, there's theatre again, what they call concert parties, actors with their faces painted setting up in the squares and clowning around. You can see them emoting in scenes of exaggerated drama, parodies of domestic situations or brawls among the common folk, fights between lovers, friends, or the weak and the strong, and when the weak one, his face twisted, collapses at the feet of the powerful one in a horrific enactment of the eternal victim, the crowd assembled around the actors bursts into uncontrollable laughter. And I imagine my friends watching the spectacle. Beno the loony walking past the scene indifferent, his newspapers under his arm, Beno lost, with his head permanently in the clouds and the shit. And I imagine Wali's mother pushing the tricycle on which her son vegetates into the crowd of spectators in the hope that it will awaken the past and some emotions in him, in the hope that her lifeless son will start to move again, to live again. And since all this is taking place at an intersection where there's a lot of traffic, I also envision Sika, more and more huge, passing by on the way back from her shopping and asking her driver to stop the car for a moment, rolling the back window down, and casting a vacant gaze at the spectacle, a tear running down her cheek.

There are concert parties, they say, but there are also more traditional theatre troupes offering a variety of plays. A theatre that makes reference to the world of a Jarry or a Soyinka before leading you elsewhere in the singular decline of a people whose last dead souls were found at an intersection in the heart of a city devastated by an earthquake, to consider nobody knows what, since, obviously, there was no life anymore. Or that other creation in which tropical kings succeeded one another on a blood-soaked throne in a very short period of time, and to get to that throne, they each had to imagine and bring about the death of the previous monarch, with trickery, plots, backstabbing, treason, informing, and murders, until the throne disappeared under a sea of blood and the last putschist king no longer knew where to sit, he had nothing left but an emptiness to sit his colonial sergeant's ass on and govern the flies and the dogs. Or that other play in which the tropical kings had gone mad, all of them, and they organized a ball where they danced with whores and virgins, and the game was to try to be the first one to contrive the death of the other madmen, to poison their lives, and the wine that flowed freely down their gullets and between the thighs of the virgins and harlots, where they were forever sticking their noses and losing their wits. And the public, surprised and rapt, shouted hurrahs. Yes, Kimi, plays like that, always in that tropical order of things that don't work.

But the most impressive of the creators who have overrun the city, I was told, is a young man known as Bob Silak, who puts on the old Marivaux classic *The Game of Love and Chance* in his own way, using amateur actors who, in spite of the chopper, the sergeant, and the Uzi, take pleasure in wooing anyone who meets their mischievous gaze. On an improvised stage in a public square, they say to a woman spectator, "I love you madly! And if you look in your mirror, you'll see that it is inevitable." And the girls in the audience go along with the game because, in spite of the fear and the permanent state of siege, it is essential to continue creating scenes and a country for love. That's what I tried to do with you, Kimi, but you must have realized very quickly that I'm one of those who can no longer invent anything, neither love nor hate. But at those times and those places where Bob Silak has his actors play, many pairs of eyes meet and many relationships are forged. People fall in love and go off to love each other until the next riot. That's the game, and at night they cling to each other until a stray bullet explodes the chest of one of them, or the cops come and pick them up to throw them in prison for good. But sometimes the stray bullet lands elsewhere than in a body, sometimes it ends its flight of death in a wall, sparing the lovers, who then can continue the game of love until the next season. And that's how life goes on back home, as in many other times and places. One lives in those rare spaces spared by the bullets.

44

As for me, in the months following my return from the camp, I lived more or less as a recluse, shut up in my bedroom in front of a big notebook in which I tried to write, a recluse because I'd lost the habit of living in the open air, in the wind from the sea or the sun in our alleys, which were too full of the friends I had just reconnected with. A kind of phobia of others and the outside world. It was hard to take up my troublemaking life with my friends where we had left off. I couldn't help thinking that, at any moment, the "shadow police" would get their hands on them, their hands, billy clubs, the hood slipped over the head, the head and entire body diving into a ditch in which the remains of other unfortunates who had been betrayed were growing cold. But time passed and nothing happened. After the riots that led to the closing of the camps, it was the status quo once again, freeze image until the next explosion, the last act that would give the apocalypse its full dimensions, its eruption of fire, screams, and death.

The country was paralysed by a general strike called by opposition parties and followed by most of the unions. The public service, the schools, and the university were closed, and the demand was that members and leaders of the military withdraw from politics. But it was hard for us to imagine the sergeant with the Uzi putting away his anger and his engines of death to go and spend the rest of his vulture's life in the calm of a barracks. The strike lasted a year, and during that time,

I saw very little of my friends. I made all kinds of excuses to avoid the outings they suggested, increasingly rare excursions into the bowels of our capital, because the desire was no longer there. My defection may have destroyed our wonderful esprit de corps, and in truth, I must say we no longer shared that unique restless spirit of dream and subversion. The first day I was reunited with my friends, I felt something like a weariness in them, as if they no longer believed in it, in spite of my return from hell.

For my father, too, there was a pause, but, refusing the immobility imposed by the strike, he would wake up at dawn and, as he had always done on days of rest, he would set up his drafting table on our terrace and start drawing plans for houses that had not been commissioned. It was as if he was afraid that things would stop, that the country would end up disappearing into a sludge of tainted earth, blood, and broken bones. He was afraid, so he continued making his drawings, and on the tracing paper would appear the streets and buildings of our improbable future. And when the embers in my mother's stove in the yard crackled as she busied herself preparing breakfast, when the burning charcoal filled the air with incandescent particles, perverse little morning stars, I was afraid. I was afraid the burning particles would fall on my father's drawings and cause them to burst into flames, reducing the work he had done to ashes.

And when I wasn't spending time silently observing my father's work, I stayed shut up in my room in front of the big notebook in which I had hesitantly started to do my first writing. Because we had gotten to know Beckett and the playwrights of our streets, I was trying to grope my way to writing a play. I remember creating pathetically naive scenes dripping with clichés of hope. I titled my play "The Country and the Roses." It was totally rosy and optimistic, because, after the camp, it was—not hard to guess—an attempt to reintegrate a ghost into a life that, little by little, would run away from him, a life now marked by a permanent shiver, a trembling of my whole carcass at the slightest unexpected sound. And when I went out, I would turn around a thousand times, because I had the feeling I was being followed, so I'd cut short my errands to return to my lair. I'm a guy of lairs and caves, with life going on over my head while I cling to my prehistoric dream of freedom. But cracks long ago started to appear in the cave, like this basement, and everything is going to tumble down on us in a rain of rocks and dust.

I never was able to find the text of that first play, I never found the country and the roses again, but I remember my disappointment on reading the final result. I had written that play in one sitting, and reading the words of happiness, I retched. It was shit that was too beautiful, too smooth, the stench removed. But shit, by definition, stinks, it churns your insides, your guts. However, little by little, in that rosy rereading of the country, Koli's face began to appear. Koli, his regular features hardened by death, his hair a dazzling white, and finally, that was the light, it was the white hair and the childlike smile of a cellmate to whom I was reading *Candide* for the tenth time. My pages were filled with Koli Lem's face, his head of light carried by a body that was drier and drier, his limbs stretching in the movement of walking. And Giacometti's *The Walking Man*, to me, was Koli, walking in the streets of a city on fire like a body without a grave, walking towards someone, a friend who has promised to find him a grave, and who has said to him, "I will always remember you." I believe I never promised Koli anything, except to try to write if I could, and finally, after months of shutting myself in, scribbling and erasing, I managed to write another play, one in which there was a dead man walking in a city on fire in search of his grave.

My father encouraged me to submit that play to some of the literary competitions that were announced on posters on the walls of the cultural centres of the capital. If you won, you could get a grant to go to Avignon, Brussels, or Limoges. I didn't win Avignon, but there was a visiting Canadian artist in our city at that time who had been on the preselection committee for one of the competitions. And when I was more and more shut up in my bedroom and least expecting it, I received a letter from that man saying he was disappointed that I hadn't won the competition. He asked what I was doing—what I was doing besides writing—and urged me to submit a new play project to him. He would, with the help of a friend who ran an institution that provided funding for artists, help me get a grant to go to Quebec. For my file for the institution as well as for my visa application, I had to have a very serious project and mention that I had come in second in a previous competition in France. We anticipated some problems getting my visa, but that didn't happen. I was free to go. And a little over a year after my return from the camp, I went away.

I went away, finally, farther than Koli had hoped. I went away accompanied by the bright shadow and the candid head of my friend, and from then on, in the streets of my new life, Koli would push me from behind to help me keep moving towards salvation. Koli, the walking man, was no longer searching for a grave where he could rest his bones. His goal now was different, to give me courage and a desire to move forward. But that horse had been out of the race for a long time, broken and shoved into a corner of a cell long before the race. And since then, only the man Koli has been walking in the streets, while the horse has been sinking deeper and deeper into the sewers, with a new identity as a rat.

45

Dawn is breaking, with bluish glints on the window. Ito Baraka is suffocating. Kimi wonders if she should make him stop dictating. He's hardly breathing anymore. Kimi again stops writing, the pen in her fist, eyes staring in front of her at the black screen of the TV.

"Let's stop, Ito. You need to rest," she whispers haltingly.

Ito props himself up on one elbow. "I need to rest? No, Kimi. Just drop it, you know very well it's all over! I've been trying to tell you for hours. There's nothing more to be done, which is why I've spent the night talking to you about Beckett and the living dead. If you'd left before now, I wouldn't have been such a bother to you. Kimi Blue, why won't you? You could have gotten out a long time ago, but no, you stayed, hoping for the absurd miracle of a resurrection of this strange creature. You blew it, my friend, it was game over at the start! What came after that was this slow rot you're seeing. How can anyone put up with that? In the name of what? Love? But maybe you're simply drowning in what I see as your fascination with the worst things in life? Your cancerous mother who saw her organs destroyed, one after the other, your alcoholic father who killed himself, your junkie friends panhandling at the intersections of the world, and who knows what else? It's time for you to think a little about yourself, Kimi Blue, you can't manage all the shit in the world! Mother Teresa, Doctor Schweitzer, they croaked in the end! She in a filthy Calcutta slum, and he in the pygmies' green hell on the shores of the Congo River! I remind you that we met in the yard behind your store, between two garbage cans. And I didn't see that as a good sign. Things were rotten from the beginning, Kimi. How many couples meet in such bizarre surroundings? You know what you have to do now? Get out! I remind you once again, at the risk of annoying you, of the role I had in Beckett's play. I was Nagg, the grumpy, crazy old man stuck in his trashcan. I would stay there in a fetal position, and from time to time, I'd lift the lid to breathe a bit, because a fetus clings to life, it wants to be born. But I don't want to, I've decided not to lift the lid anymore to breathe the tainted air. Let's turn the page, Kimi Blue. What do you say? Have you made a decision? What is it? You're staying? No, no, get the hell out! But before you leave, let me confess my shame at having sold out my friends in the purgatory of a torture chamber. If I'd held out, nothing would have happened to them. Because how can you explain the fact that all three were reduced to useless remnants of humanity, to that vegetative state in which they can no longer do anything but blink their eyes powerlessly at the changing seasons? Accidents, unfortunate coincidences, bad luck, you might say. But I can't help thinking that the driver who ran over Wali was acting under orders, that Beno became a loony after a violent confrontation with a member of a shadowy militia tasked with settling scores with all those little shit disturbers whose names were on a blacklist for revenge, that the colonel who married Sika did so under orders, with express instructions to stuff her like a goose so she would swell and swell until she exploded within the gilded walls of her prison villa, that Nivaquine was given orders to eliminate Koli, who had dared to organize my escape. That's it, Kimi, no doubt about it, don't try to convince me otherwise! I've known it for a long time, and because there's nothing to be done about this terrible truth, I giggle like a survivor after the moment of euphoria and I drink to the vegetative health of my friends! And at night, I close my eyes in the hope of being released from my burdensome carcass, I try, like Koli Lem's flying men, to free myself from the birdlime of memories by spreading my burned survivor's wings above the clouds. I try but invariably fail to conquer the skies of oblivion or detachment, and I fall back down heavily into this corrupt, rotten body. If you insist on helping me, here's what you should do, Kimi. Find some of those hot peppers that set your tongue and your epidermis on fire, and rub my body with them when you see that I've left it for a night flight. That way, my spirit will not dare come back to its overheated former abode, and from up above, I'll be able to see my carcass slowly waste away like the bodies forgotten in the street after a riot."

46

Kimi Blue has stopped listening to him. The first bird of the morning is making its song heard. After calling the ambulance, she asks Ito Baraka the question that has been burning her lips. She wants to know about Koli Lem. "How did Koli lose his eyes?"

"Starting in the second week of his detention, they sat him in a chair."

"To torture him?"

"Yes. In a chair facing the sun."

"Didn't he close his eyes?"

"He had to keep them open."

"Why?"

"To look at the sun."

"That's horrible. And what if he closed them?"

"If he closed his eyes, the guard standing behind him would grab him by the hair, pull his head back, and open his eyelids with his fingers."

"He could have looked to the side or somewhere else."

"The sky was filled with that cruel light. And when he resisted, another soldier would crush Koli's toes with his boots."

"So he kept looking at the sun."

"For three long weeks."

"All day long?"

"Yes. Until all the lights went out."

"Was he sad?"

"A little."

"A little?"

"Just a little. Because everything around was ugly anyway. There was nothing beautiful to look at, except the curves of the whore who came once a month to offer her ass to the corporals."

"It's true, you said that woman wasn't ugly."

"Right."

"Nice breasts?"

"Yes. Once she arrived at the camp in a transparent top. In the evening, in our cell, I . . . "

" . . . pleasured yourself."

"And on cold nights, I'd go at it again. You had to hang on, one way or another."

"You had books."

"You're getting on my nerves, Kimi Blue."

"Okay, I'll stop. Should we get ready? The ambulance will be here soon."

"No. We're not going to the hospital. We're going to sleep, to play-act at spending a normal night. And just as I've been doing for three months, I'm going to bury my head between your breasts until dawn. Like an old fool who in spite of everything still clings to life."

Aylmer (Quebec), Lomé, Cape Town,
June 2011–April 2013

EDEM AWUMEY was born in Lomé, Togo. He is the author of three previous novels, *Port-Melo* (2006), which won the prestigious Grand prix littéraire d'Afrique noire; *Les pieds sales* (2009), which was a finalist for the Prix Goncourt in France; and *Rose déluge* (2011). The English translation of *Les pieds sales*, *Dirty Feet* (2011), was selected for the Dublin Impac Award. In 2006 Awumey was selected to be a literary protégé to the renowned Moroccan writer Tahar Ben Jelloun. Edem Awumey currently lives in Gatineau, Quebec.